THE YEAR
OF THE
HOT JOCK

·

AND OTHER
STORIES

BOOKS BY IRVIN FAUST

SHORT STORY COLLECTIONS
Roar Lion Roar
The Year of the Hot Jock

NOVELS
The Steagle
The File on Stanley Patton Buchta
Willy Remembers
Foreign Devils
A Star in the Family
Newsreel

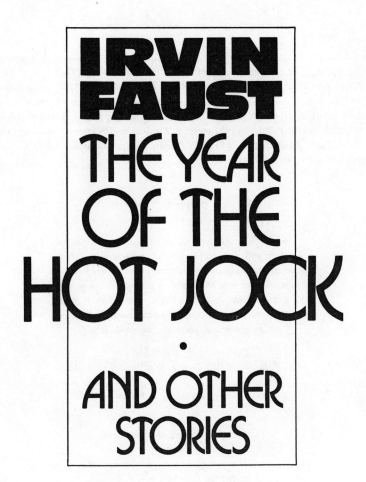

IRVIN FAUST

THE YEAR OF THE HOT JOCK

·

AND OTHER STORIES

A William Abrahams Book
E. P. DUTTON □ NEW YORK

Of the stories in this collection, "The Year of the Hot Jock" appeared in *Confrontation* (Spring 1985), "Operation Buena Vista" in *The Paris Review* (Fall 1965), "The Dalai Lama of Harlem" in *The Sewanee Review* (Spring 1964), "The Double Snapper" in *Esquire* (December 1965), "Simon Girty Go Ape" in *The Transatlantic Review* (Vol. 21, 1966), "Gary Dis-Donc" in *The Northwest Review* (Summer 1967), "Melanie and the Purple People Eaters" in *The Atlantic* (December 1981) and *Prize Stories, The O. Henry Awards, 1983*, and "Bunny Berigan in the Elephants' Graveyard" in *Action/Image* (Spring 1985).

Published in the United States by
E. P. Dutton, 2 Park Avenue, New York, N.Y. 10016

Library of Congress Cataloging in Publication Data

Faust, Irvin.
The year of the hot jock and other stories.
"A William Abrahams book."
Contents: The year of the hot jock—Bar bar bar—
Operation Buena Vista—[etc.]
I. Title.
PS3556.A97Y4   1985   813'.54   85-4422

ISBN: 0-525-24343-7
Published simultaneously in Canada
by Fitzhenry and Whiteside, Ltd.

Designed by Mark O'Connor

COBE

10 9 8 7 6 5 4 3 2 1

First Edition

This book is
for
Allison Baer.

CONTENTS

THE YEAR OF THE HOT JOCK
1

BAR BAR BAR
29

OPERATION BUENA VISTA
63

THE DALAI LAMA OF HARLEM
85

THE DOUBLE SNAPPER
109

SIMON GIRTY GO APE
137

GARY DIS-DONC
151

MELANIE AND THE PURPLE PEOPLE EATERS
167

BUNNY BERIGAN IN THE ELEPHANTS' GRAVEYARD
191

THE YEAR OF THE HOT JOCK

Had a great day. Four-bagger at Aqueduct. Tenth time in my career. Almost nailed two more. Lost one on photo, lost one on bob of the nose. They say you can't win them all. Who are they? I say why not? On way home bought Ramona fur wrap, Olga bracelet, Lorenzo Walkman . . .

Inform them as watch me kick in fourth winner have to ride Stir Krazy Hialeah. In Bougainvillea, Jan. 30. Ramona responds with her mourning face, kids understand 100%. Learn a lot from kids. But what can she say after fur wrap? Not much.

Catch 8 A.M. La Guardia. Have to rescue Jeff Kahn Hialeah. Tough but fair trainer who got a bad trip from Ben Gotch last time out. Jock can lose for Jeff, but must lose good. Can always win bad, but better lose good.

Eastern pilot comes through with real nice trip. Relax with *Racing Form,* beats mysteries, plus learn something. Know it all, but always learning. An extra. Full of extras. Over Delaware notice blonde next seat peeking over. Not unusual. Over Virginia give her a break. Pardon me, you into horses? Oh yes, she's into horses. Loves the gorgeous creatures. Gorgeous but dumb as shit; don't tell her that. Agree, some lovely animals. Likes words like lovely from a man. Sensitive. Terrific parlay, strength and sensitive. She just knows has seen me somewhere, maybe Gulfstream, Calder, Belmont. Well, guess you have, happen to be Pablo Diaz. Have to slip that in fast, they can't tell us apart—Hernandez, Cordero, Santiago, Diaz. Rings a great bell, she saw me win Woodward Belmont, beautiful race. Can't argue, I stole it.

When she gets up to go to john see she goes easy five-nine and velvety all over. Not young, but fine condition. When returns tell her contact me Fontainebleau if care for a box for Bougainvillea, very decent race. Expect to do rather well. Modest. Goes with sensitive. Gives me soft, velvet look, just might take you up on that. Forget it, she's hooked.

Jeff meets plane, very jumpy, hustles me out to track. Stir Krazy still a nut job, been that way since he hit the ground, but can run like Slew on uppers when in the mood. That's his problem, mood. Take him for a ride and croon Spanish lullaby and he gentles right down. Remember that from two years ago Turf Paradise. Another extra. Inform Jeff his horse will be fine, he sighs, calms right down. Have to play trainers like horses.

Check into Fontainebleau. They go into their act. Yes, Mr. Diaz, of course not, Mr. Diaz, anything else, Mr. Diaz? All bullshit, but love it. Earned every bob of the head, every open door, paid some heavy dues. No brothers, uncles in the business like Jeff. Thirteen years ago. Thirteen. Just another dark monkey-on-a-stick. Toss a whip, hit ten of us. Hole up on a straw mattress in grooms' quarters. Live on white bread and OJ. Whothehell is this kid Diaz? Eighty million in purses later, Jock of the Year, a Wood, a Woodward, a Travers, a Preakness, ho hum, maybe they know who is Diaz, yes?

Hit the big round bed for two hours. Action, rest, action, rest, law of nature. Phone. Bounce up, walk slow, one guess. Helena Stadler, velvet blonde from plane. Accept your generous offer. Smile at phone, my pleasure, *hasta la vista.* Little Spanish, not too much. Call Jeff. Set her up in owner's box, he's fishing for tuna off Lauderdale. Jeff: Pablo, please don't screw around till after the race. Relax, Mr. Kahn, I know my priorities. Can hear his sigh, he loves those words.

Call down to room service. Order filet mignon, baked potato, the works. Tip kid ten, autograph menu for him.

Eat very careful, very slow. Then very careful, very slow, walk to john, flip up whole goddam thing. Ah, still got it. Sensational will power. You got that, you got it all. Providing God bless you with hands of steel, a brain, fantastic ability. Thank you, God. Gargle Listerine.

Call Miami Motors, order Mercedes. Tip kid fifty. Drive slow and easy through city to track. Cuba all the way. Ten years ago. Green kid on the move. Win the Flamingo, meet Ramona. Sixteen years old and don't know a horse from a chicken. But busting out all over. And backside never stops flicking at me. And same size. Five and change. Don't realize can handle tall stuff till I win Preakness three years later. Don't count. Did her number on me. But give her this: Ramona very religious. Oh yes. Gives me many glimpses heaven, but won't open gates till she gets me in church . . .

Hialeah not what it used to be, what is? But still lakes and thick grass and sensational birds. They don't know racing, but great for tourists. Walk into jocks' quarters, hand out friendly hellos. They interrupt their ping pong and poker, mumble hello, track me around the room the way I used to watch Hartack and Baeza. Love it.

Walk out to Mr. Gracklin's box. Owner Stir Krazy, poor bastard. Poor rich bastard. Delighted I'm here. Me too, Mr. Gracklin. Mean it. He likes Spanish jocks. Well, he likes winners.

Next day Jan. 30. Come into feature after riding fourth, sixth race. Win fourth from here to West Palm, nice price. Finish third in sixth on nag who chucks it final 16th. Off at 2–1 and crowd blames me, but Jeff don't. Knows this horse hates to win, professional runner-up. But hope springs eternal, especially when the trainer got Diaz.

Check certain box. Yes, she's there. In large floppy hat,

with guy: chestnut tan, wearing cabana shirt. Back to priorities.

Bougainvillea goes nine and half furlongs. Mile and then some. Krazy got sire to go distance, but mother a nut. Up to Diaz, wipe her out of his head. Jeff talks, I listen. Always follow orders 100%. Not my fault if orders are rotten. He tells me take Krazy back and keep him sane. Move off final turn. These orders very okay.

Do just that. Hold him easy but firm. He behaves, knows he can trust me. Come off turn, show him the whip, only show. The saved-up power switches on. He fires whoooosh. I hand-ride him in by length and a half. Have worked harder in sweat box. Good ones alway make it look easy. Flip my stick to grinning groom, hop down, pose in winner's circle with Jeff, Mr. Gracklin. As I turn toward jocks' room he slips me a crisp grand.

Change, take my sweet time. Walk out to Mercedes. Note on wiper with Helena Stadler's number. Take some more time, then call. Drive slow, careful, wind up party in Boca. Sweet little condo, part of her divorce deal. She introduces me all around, they eat me up. Few won bundle on me. Circulate. Polite. When asked for tip, say Pleasant Colony sure thing to win Derby. Always big hit, plus message: Don't pump Diaz.

Crowd thins out around 3:30. At 4:20 just me and the tanned guy from box left. He's watching TV as Helena and prime guest go upstairs. She informs me her first time with a jock, but says believes in variety of experience. Can't argue with that. She likes to play horsey. Nothing very new there. Up and out at 6:37. Quiet, tan guy shakes my hand, wishes me luck. Not a bad guy but leads a strange life. Watching TV as I walk out to catch 8 A.M. back to NY. After action, sleep. All the way.

Ramona has to greet me with problems. Don't even ask did I come out of race sound? Always check the horse, why not a top jock? Okay, now what? Lorenzo and Olga. Fresh mouths, get off their case. Just log three thousand miles, ride my ass off, make two grand plus, and this my reward. Tell her, politely, kids are her department. Informs me, not so politely, they're 50% mine. Bite my tongue; Panama woman never give me that routine. Ramona's family skipped out of Cuba one length ahead of Castro. She didn't have a pot to sit on till she nailed King Pablo. Now she gives me long division. Thank you, Fidel.

Lecture kids in English. Strictly English. Tell them I do it all for them, expect loyalty in return. If mother sometimes don't make sense, nobody is perfect. Ground them both two weeks. Tears could fill up Atlantic Ocean. Make it one week.

Steaming so hard, go out next day and ride three winners Aqueduct. In rain, cold, mud. Work through five pairs of goggles in sixth. Feel human again. On way home, order moped for Lorenzo, 8-inch color TV for Olga.

Now my agent. Hy Platkin. Complains I don't consult enough on big races. Just a phone call, catching a plane, seeya. Whole world complains and all I do is make them money. But explain, politely, Jeff Kahn in tough spot and I always bail out old friends. Anyhow, won and we both make out okay. Hy not the hustler he once was, but he spotted Diaz, so he don't have to be. Earned him 200 big ones last year. But Pablo Diaz is a U.S. Marine—always faithful. Remind him. Hy relaxes, lights up. How about I go back down to Florida Feb. 13 for Donn Handicap Gulfstream? Can get me on that nice 3-year-old colt, Wineglo. He's a good one, Hy. You telling me? And Lester Pawkins wants you, Paul. Lovely old man. Spotted me Government

Riding School Panama. Liked my hands, head, way I sat a horse. My style. Even then, the Diaz style. Brought me to Florida, rest is history.

I'm a Marine elephant, always faithful and never forget. You got it, Hy. Tell Mr. Pawkins Pablo Diaz ride for him on the moon. Hy pats my face, father never did that once, walks off to do some relaxed hustling.

Ride splendid into February Big A. Shooting for eleven million this year, off to big start. Freeze nuts off, so what? Maybe the hot shot bug boys learn a lesson when they see Diaz pound through snow, rain, mud, come back for more. Maybe they learn; don't bet your eating money.

Day before Donn Handicap call school, tell them, politely, Lorenzo has virus, take him with me to airport. Begs me go to Florida, never saw me ride there. True. Doing nothing important in school. Wellll. Write a composition, My Father and Me and a Horse. Done.

We fly first class, behave myself entire trip. Got my kid with me. Land and call Ramona first thing. Screams so loud, phone jumps. Are you *crazy*? Beautiful trip. *Crazy.* Thought I'd take him off your hands few days; should learn the business. Screaming louder now, people looking: he's going to college, he don't need your business. Stay calm, not easy: I didn't go to college and I can buy one or two, don't worry, I called his school. She hangs up. Can you make them happy?

Rent new Imperial at airport and drive to Gulfstream. Love me in Gulfstream. Introduce big-eyed Lorenzo all around and ask assistant trainer Karl Witkin keep an eye on kid, show him a thing or two while I take care of business. Sure, Pablo. They take off around backstretch, kid seventh heaven. Get this at Harvard?

Mr. Pawkins getting on and takes my arm as we walk down shed row, talk about old, happy days. Had a Derby winner hundred years ago; Pablo, one more classic winner and I die happy.

Maybe it's Wineglo. Maybe. Long, long way to paydirt. But Mr. Pawkins a pro. He discovered me. Look his baby over. Smallish colt. Chestnut. Pretty blaze. *Very* well formed, tight, front legs out of same hole. Mr. P. says he runs with his head down, like he's looking for uncashed tickets. Love that. Give me those low runners, they mean business. Can't stand a high head, run like trotters. Abnormal. Decent but not great sire and dam. He's a maybe, nice maybe, but maybe. Get acquainted. Say this, a real gentleman. Could mean something. Or nothing. Will meet some older horses in Donn. Learn something. Maybe. Trainer Tim Seelen. Gives me polite hello. Wanted someone like Fell or even Shoe. But Mr. Pawkins one owner who says this, not that, you do this. So from Tim polite hello.

Pick up Lorenzo, still sky-high, drive to hotel Hallendale, check in, make him take hot bath calm down, feed him first class. Never make it as jock, too many vitamins, maybe a trainer. Or first dark president NY Racing Assoc. Tuck him in, click TV. Be back soon, sonny, have to talk strategy with Mr. Pawkins and Tim. Eyes tiny slits as I tiptoe out.

Saddle up, point Imperial at Bal Harbor. Twenty minutes later relaxing 110th Street, thirty-fifth-floor condo overlooking smooth, calm ocean. With Ginny Gottlieb. Who listens to all my sadness and does nothing but nod her head and keep quiet. Whips up neat, nutritious salad. Then takes care of *me*.

Get back to hotel 3 A.M. Lorenzo in dreamland with late late show. Turn it down but not off, likes a voice in his room. Catch five hours real sleep. If felt better, I'd see a doctor.

Next day just ride feature. Set kid up with Mr. Pawkins. Instant hit. His grandchildren spoiled rotten. Check in and change. Silks orange and black, colors Princeton College. Left after two years to enter real world, but still loyal. Respect that, common bond. And college didn't hurt him. Report to Tim in paddock. He talks fast but good. Wants a wire job. Nod. Have very respectful nod. Paddock judge gives us Riders up! Best two words English language. Step out to post parade, back to gate.

Give Tim his wire job, win by a neck. Hold him on rail entire trip. Rail golden. Like inside my head. Tim can't play with that. Only Diaz can.

Lorenzo jumping out of pants next to me winner's circle, along with Mr. P. and Tim. Very good thing kid see his father a hero. Make sure never be a faggot. My case, had uncles who stepped in. Had to. My old man hardly ever home. Worked all the time. Shoe factory Balboa. When he got home, never talked. Not a bad man, just tired. And no hero. Didn't even argue when Mr. Pawkins wanted me to go to States. Should have. Then give in. Silence. Now they own the canal.

Ginny waves to me from her box. Back in hotel, bouquet of flowers. Someone giving *me* something. Two-day vacation. Catch plane back to NY. Beautiful sleep. Get home and Lorenzo can't stop talking. Olga can't stop crying. Why does he go and I stay? That's the way it is. But *why?* Kids born that word in their mouth. From Ramona finally get something. Closed gates.

Terrific week. Typical. Fifteen winners 6 days. Buy Ramona Zuni necklace for 3 thou. Loves that Indian stuff, makes her feel like a princess. Loosens her up for her prince. Pablo, the Prince of Great Neck. Peace.

Hy gets me on Sugar Blue for Barbara Fritchie Bowie last week February. Grade III Stake but worth a hundred bigs. Sugar supposed to be best filly since Risk. But just like Ramona, blows hot and cold. Run out of your picture one race, act like having her period the next. Trainer Abe Pilky. Talks with marbles in mouth, but I understand him. Thinks change of jocks could help. Might have a point. Red-haired stewardess checks me out, but don't blink; too short. Some trip, take off, fire, land, wham.

Out at track meet Abe and darling Sugar. One look, all I need. Hates people. You can change jocks, can't change their heads. Don't tell Abe. He jabbers, I nod. Adds up to, don't let her loaf; if have to, kick the shit out of her. Sugar looks at me, I look at her. Sure.

Dwells at gate. Studying the crowd. Finally consents to run. Work her like crazy, finally in gear after first half. Switch hit her entire final eighth, get her up to 3rd. Far as she'll go, that's it. Miracle get show money. Crowd gets on jock, what else is new? Abe disappointed, but says maybe we get em next time. Next time he tries Migliore or Cordero. Good luck baby.

Fly away home. Ramona extremely considerate. Likes it when I lose now and then. Long as I'm in the money. Cooks up tremendous Cuban dinner, paella, beans, the works. Tell her she knows I can't eat fat. Answers can't kill you once in a while. It can, but don't want jeers or tears. Shovel it in. Don't even flip. Sweat box, here I come. What I do for peace. Pope Pablo . . .

Mar. 6 and we drive to Keystone in my green Mercedes, green for all my lettuce, me and Hy. Hit seventy on Jersey

Turnpike, could hit a hundred. Easy. If not Paul the Great might settle for Richard Petty, racing is racing, except on four wheels it's snow white. Maybe buy way in when retire, $ make me Pale the Great . . .

At Keystone win 50 thou Cotillion on big ugly filly, Outamyway, so easy almost boring except a win and nice $ always interesting. Tap her just once, wave stick like it's sugar cane. She fires like a moon shot, bye bye baby.

On way back stop off Atlantic City, blow fifteen hundred, easy come, so on, so forth. But find a cushion. Connect with waitress who has so much might be illegal. Goes six-one easy, amaze her with speed and power in compact package, by time I leave has dropped "cute" routine which I hate, so pretty fair night after all. Hymie drives us home while I curl up in back and sleep like brand new foal . . .

Pick up Big A where I left off, but hit a snag, or envy, or both. Set down Mar. 10 for tough but 100% honest ride against new bug boy, everybody's darling. Never protect me like that when I come up, now they stand on head to protect every new hot shot, even Spanish, *especially* Spanish. Dear Public, no prejudice here.

Sit around for entire week, nothing to do except work some horses, listen to Ramona and kids on phone. Plus stuff face and go nuts. Get so crazy absolutely necessary get some relief. Not what you think, I *do* have other outlets. Drive into Manhattan, 114th Street, Third Avenue, residence of best and oldest friend in U.S.A. Rafael Laguna. Who came to states together with yrs truly way back when, is true blue while I am likewise ditto. Rafael the greatest shortstop in Panama, hell, all Central America, even at five-three, another Freddie Patek, better glove. Reached top minors, up to Oneonta, that's it. Couldn't hit change-up, fastball. Not even satin glove carry that, or great arm. One summer, whoosh, down and so long *béisbol,* you no so good to him. But Happiness Inc. Blows all his money on horses, never complains, always smiling, ballplayer's beer-belly. Maybe knows something I don't know . . . ?

Sit in his flaking, secondhand kitchen while his latest woman who could use the sweat box sits inside and jumps when he says jump. Breaks out some real beer, the light stuff makes him sick. I relax first time all week, Rafael never even asks for a tip, that's friendship baby. Ramona can't stand him, real plus for Rafael. She says he got eyes for her. Have told her a hundred times she's nuts, watches too much "General Hospital" where everybody screwing everybody. She tells me she knows men's eyes. Tell her that's all she better know or she's a dead Cuban, but she's dreaming. Dreams okay long as she don't wake up and perform. Anyway Rafael likes them fat and sloppy and accommodating. Ramona just make one out of three: fat. Beautiful evening, beer and old times. Can't sit still in Great Neck, loose as a goose el Barrio. Figure that out, I write a book . . .

Get home very late, tell her had to work out Jack La Lanne's. Pablo Diaz got more stories than loser at track. But idea always makes sense. Like this one. Next day hit sweat box for three hours, hit it every day left in suspension. Cut down to 113, not great but ride better at 113 than Joe Blow at 90. First day back got head of steam like horse coming into Derby. Win four, in money five, give you a piece of something every race if you play jocks. Hot jocks. Hot *jock.* Crowd even applauds on fourth winner, 12–1 shot. Don't mean a thing, crowd applaud Hitler he kicks in 12–1 shot.

Pablo the Great is back, life is life again. Trainers get

on line. Hymie's phone rings more than Olga's. Consults me, he better. Pick and choose, get some nice horses, make them nicer. Some nice races, especially one. Dominion Day, Woodbine, north of the border, 75 thou, Mar. 20. Connections get screwed up, so fly Toronto same morning, check in with Rip Kelly who almost has heart attack thinking I won't show. Buy him drink at airport, another on the way, talk low and calm and tell him all about his horse: gelding, Bay Rummy, old friend, rode him Laurel as a four-year-old, Rip leans back, sighs. Sits up, says he's six now, then was then, now is now. Does he still run like he's chasing his *cojones?* Sits back, I know his horse . . .

Race goes distance of ground, mile and an eighth. Take firm hold, he's strong as Tarzan, shoulders ache like bad tooth, but strategy works. Two apprentices kill each other off while we lay fifth, off final turn old pro goes wide, circles field, we win by one. Rip says I'm the best, I say one of the best, he says the best. Don't argue.

Before dinner call Ramona, tell her catch me 11-o'clock news, answers sure and lets kids stay up. So amazed go out and buy her Zuni bracelet. Then celebrate with Shana O'Toole, hostess in hotel restaurant, we go back five Dominion Days, terrific hostess.

Fly home 6 A.M. Presents for everybody.

I'm a bitch April. Recapture $ lead Aqueduct, number 3 in wins. Redhot bug boy number 1, they ride every race, weight allowance, so why not? However, develop certain problem, although real nice one: Which of two Derby horses gets Diaz? Offered Wineglo by Mr. Pawkins and Scoliosis, California horse. Loyal Mr. P., but his little nag loves germs and accidents, catches this, steps on that. If superstitious (I'm not), say evil eye got him. Out on coast,

Scoliosis going great this year, big, healthy, solid, excellent paper, daddy won Arlington Classic, mama daughter Preakness winner. Trainer Arnold Lewisohn, smart man, likes strong jock on strong horse, guess who? Tell Hy. Rocks on eight-hundred-dollar Tony Lama boots, okay boss, damn right okay. Call down to Mr. Pawkins, break tough news, takes it like real thoroughbred, good luck Pablo. Almost change mind, don't, once I move, I move. Tell Ramona it's California. Sigh. After ninth race Aqueduct call Brenda Burlington, English actress hooked on horses and dark, strong jocks. Jock. California, here he comes.

April 10. Santa Anita Derby mile and an eighth. Scoliosis rank in paddock. Determined show NY star who's boss. Hates gate, almost kicks it to Catalina, hands almost raw meat by time we break. Get off dead last, bust behind to crank him up, finally fires and we close to 2nd. Winner Fat Bat, another Derby hopeful. His jock Cal Jones, King of the Koast. Swivels head at wire, informs me this ain't your turf, *señor*. Give me another 16th, even with this bad actor and I show him whose turf it is. Don't say a word. Crowd takes care of that. *Two* words: you bum.

We got trouble, Arnold and me. Scoliosis starts limping on way back to barn. Big healthy brute looks at me like I did it. Arnold not so happy either, avoids my eyes, tells press we'll know story tomorrow. Reporters look at me: Thanks a lot, New York. Smile, look back, drop dead.

Change, meet Brenda Burlington our private spot, drive out Holmby Hills her BMW. Still not talking, losing hurts, losing on favorite kills me, my horse comes up lame, kills me dead. Brenda real track fan, understands. Lot like Ginny, only bigger. Says very quiet, you gave him a great trip, big bum lucky to get place money. By time we reach her house, almost smiling, checking out Technicolor profile.

Small party that night, intimate, exclusive, suntans, penny loafers, dresses down to the south pole. Producers, few directors, some movie stars who'd love to be in real life, never make it. Loosen up on coke, sound like horses blowing out, only blow in. One of them in a custom shirt and new nose challenges me to hand wrestle. Pin pathetic bastard five seconds, toss him in pool. Loves it, toss him in six times. Smash hit, they all love it. Line up, toss them all in, keep on tossing, can't get enough, me, me, me. Pissing in their custom jeans, still me, me, happy to oblige, work off loss and limpy Scoliosis, one terrific bitch. Toss for two hours till Brenda blows cop's whistle, yells CUT. Beg, plead, Brenda one tough limey, cut and out, the man is tired, he ran a big race today. Shake my hand, file out, wet but happy, two girls slip me phone numbers, I play dumb, Brenda watching, one jealous star, don't screw with her man.

Alone beside pool, like to tell me something. In that Brit voice, soft, cool, opposite Ramona, tells me only man she knows a bitch without coke or ludes. Inform her losing does that, she says fine, take out frustration on Great Britain, we have no business in Malvinas anyway. Don't give a shit about Malvinas, don't say so, she can have them, but take care of frustration, God Save the Queen, wind up in pool, playing sea horsey. Win that one.

Next morning send her to studio happy, borrow third or fourth car, report to track. Should have known, Scoliosis bowed tendon, most likely out of Derby. Give him best dirty look, walk away, call Hy, tell him. He has great news, Wineglo training splendid, entered Bluegrass Keeneland, prepping for Derby. All I need. Big, tough nag breaks down, tender lambchop breezes, call Brenda, California there he goes.

Catch plane to NY, watch movie starring first guy tossed in pool. Private eye, hardest bitch LA, three gorgeous women. Only real laugh whole goddam trip.

Home sweet home, Ramona into number, strokes me for losing, real pal, so nice want to belt her. Starts cooking like back in Havana. Ask her if trying to kill golden goose, answers have to keep strength up, answer back feed that BS to brother Carlos, biggest leech U.S.A. Snaps at me, always pick on brother, can't help if got bad back. Got bad head, Ramona, bang, off to races. Much better, she winds up crying, kids watching show, love our fights. Tell them do some goddam homework, they grin each other, walk upstairs. Take firm hold of self, tell her okay, turn off waterfall, let's go out. Jump into Mercedes, drive to Miracle Mile, Manhasset, spend fortune, ten dresses, shoes, underwear, Navajo necklace, smiling like Carlos when slip him two hundred. That mile some miracle. Drive home, make her doubly happy, make that the triple. More f'ing this weekend than Secretariat with full stud book.

Back in saddle Aqueduct, win long, win short, win. Pass two million mark, but still not happy, still don't have Derby horse, start to get that sinking heart never get one. Hy lands Northern Dancer nag for Wood, Stickum, real disappointment till now. Trainer, owner figure Diaz magic turn him around. Forget to inform Stickum. In contention to head of stretch, flat tire, says hell with this, dead last. Diaz players deliver expert opinion. Diaz delivers back. Picked up TV, every smartass every channel delivers lecture on obligation to public. Deliver back in interview, papers love it, back-page headlines. Hy says please shut flapping face, tell him f you too, head for sweat box, Rafael . . .

Just as feared, knew, Wineglo wins Bluegrass. By two and a half, no contest. Goes to Derby favorite, Ben Gotch up. Fat Bat, Cal Jones up, second choice, almost g.d. conspiracy. Scoliosis back home, so is Diaz. Okay, ride like hell, win, so long Kentucky, see you next year. Hy forgives me, says great adjustment kid, he's right, and so get my reward, must be moral there: just as accept fate, terrific news—Wineglo blows Derby! Correction, Ben Gotch blows it, horrible trip. 17th heaven. Not even in money, 18th heaven. Fat Bat wins it, and if can't take Cal Jones, still makes my day. Hy jumping out of Polo suit: Call Lester Pawkins, inform him available, tell him no way. Mr. P. class act, loyal even to lousy jock, sit tight, trainers different story. Nursed on mustard, especially Tim Seelen, just hang around phone . . .

Call comes in three days. No way it won't. Tim first, then Mr. Pawkins. Would I take Wineglo for Preakness? Smile into phone, take sweet time. Do it for you, Mr. Pawkins. Hy watching, listening, shaking head. Pablo, you taught me something. He's right, buy him dinner.

Fly down Baltimore. Mr. Pawkins sees me, sheds ten years. Even Tim almost human. Wineglo Wineglo. If had wings be angel. In spite of bad trip, came out of Derby sound and happy. Gallop him on Thursday, sing pretty, but let him know boss is back. Gets message, runs like oiled satin. Inform Mr. Pawkins he's ready, I'm ready, both ready. Takes off another five years. Lovely man. Call Laurie Willston Silver Spring, tell her buy some champagne, *Piper*, keep ready, man is back. Drive to motel, need quiet night.

Walk into lobby, fatguy jumps up, surprise, surprise. Rafael. Whathehell you doing here? Wishing my old friend *buena fortuna*. Thank you Rafe, but no beer tonight, need my beauty rest. Sure, sure, shakes my hand, says go get em tiger, turns, turns back, oh you got a minute? Okay yeah a minute, only a minute, but no beer. Grin, promise kid.

Walk to room, sit, he don't look so good, face red and blotchy, maybe switched to cheap wine, reach for wallet, peel off hundred, hold it out. Shakes his head. Go on, take it, Wineglo win it easy, gift to old supportive friend. Hy likes that word, supportive. Keeps on shaking his head, have to admit pleased, dumb proud bastard.

Listen, he says fast and jerky, don't win.

Stare, open mouth, close, open. Did I hear what I heard?

Don't win, Paul.

Face goes hot, keep voice down. Soft, low: This horse can't miss, Rafe.

Eyes stop shifting gears, voice levels off. You got the hands, Paulie, you can do it.

Don't answer, not yet, maybe he exits while he can. Sits there, not going anywhere. Hy once told me: In this world anything can happen. Think of that, finally say it: Rafael, you asking me to pull my horse?

I'm asking you not to kill him to win.

You asking me to pull him?

Don't be so damn technical.

I like to be technical. Are you?

Okay, if you wanna put it that way, okay yes.

Oh Jesus, Rafe, ohjesuschrist.

Get up, turn on TV. Stare at picture, picture stares back, turn it off. Look at my old friend. Who's into you, Rafe?

Never mind that.

You dumb sonuvabitch, you ask *me* to pull and tell me not to mind who's pulling *you*?

Yeah, that's what I'm tellin you. Listen, Pablo, I got a chance to make a big score, pick up my broad and move to Connecticut.

What's wrong with 114th Street?

Ah Paulie, don't give me that shit, not the kid from Great Neck.

Can't believe this, can't believe this . . .

You'll do it, won't you kid?

Do not believe this . . .

Believe it baby.

Look at my old friend who hates el Barrio. How much they dangle?

You mean how much is my score?

Yes.

You come in second, I collect 40 big ones.

And they make 10 million, you dumb sonuvabitch.

Shrug. That's their lookout, I get mine.

You sure?

I'm sure.

How hard they leaning, Rafe?

I tolyou, never mind that, it's a free country, I'm doin it on my own free will.

Very democratic.

That's right, Pablo. Hundred grand for you kid.

Stare at blank TV. Don't look, but tell him, I didn't hear you, Rafe. He says, we go back a long ways baby. I didn't hear you, go back to New York, tell your boys I'm stupid, tell them Mr. Pawkins my illegitimate father and can't screw him, tell them anything, but get the hell out of here.

Gets up, very calm, very cool, very collected, holds out hand. I shake my head. Says sure Pablo, anything you want babe, shrugs, walks out.

Do thousand goddam push-ups before get some goddam sleep.

Preakness. Wineglo ready, Diaz ready, odds ready, 2–1 along with Fat Bat. Outside hole, Fat Bat inside. Break good, Bat breaks great, zooms to three-length lead, holds most of it to head of stretch. Show Wineglo whip, grunt. He fires, pulls Bat back. Tough, so is Cal Jones, whacking his horse like hates him. Slow, sure, comes back, tail, withers, head, we're Affirmed and Alydar. Head to head, nose to nose, the wire. Wineglo turns into Alydar, we lose by that nose.

Mr. Pawkins real pro, ran a fine race Pablo, don't blame yourself. Never blame myself, but fact is fact, we lose. Expect worst from Tim, but must have got his orders from boss: Nice race, Paul, horse came out of it sound, we go for Belmont. Shake Cal Jones' hand, ran great, he did, but we'll be back, maybe different ending. Be my guest, he says, love those comebacks; he can't say thank you?

Call Laurie Willston, tell her forget champagne, sorry can't make it, see you next year, hang up, get into car, drive back motel, check out fast, catch shuttle NY, take taxi to 114th and Third.

Rafael happy as baby colt discovering legs, acts like just made Yankees. Belly out to here. Gives me his special friend hug, says I knew you'd do it baby.

I didn't do a thing, my horse lost.

Sure Paulie . . . Breaks out some Molson, his happy beer. Tell him not drinking tonight.

Okay. Pulls cigar box out of table drawer, opens it, bills with rubber bands, lousy private eye movie. For you, Paulie.

Shove it, Rafael.

Smiles, nods, slips box into drawer, glances into bedroom, his woman watching TV, slugs some beer.

One more time, he says; my old best friend.

The Belmont?

You got it, another 100 g's for Diaz.

And 40 for you?

Hey 45 baby.

Asshole, get out *now,* Rafe.

Why?

Don't you *comprende*—understand—*any*thing? I should have turned you in for the Preakness.

Sure, just do it natural, last one was perfect.

Spin so fast get dizzy, slam out, walk downtown, through park, beg somebody try number on me, break his back, one cat approaches near Central Park West, stops, examines, walks past whistling. Get home 3 A.M. Ramona waiting up. Tell her gethehell to bed *now,* don't say a goddam thing about losing. About face, upstairs, not one word. Sit in kitchen till dawn over Great Neck. Finally get up, walk to john. Take one of her goddam sleeping pills.

Aqueduct winds up, move over Belmont. Head crazy, body sane, keep winning, nothing stops that, nothing. But head keeps working, says same thing, over, over, over: Friend does this to me, friend, *best* friend, to me, to me . . . Think I go nuts if think it one more time, think it one more time, therefore must make move, if Diaz goes nuts, no longer Diaz. Impossible idea.

Go to stewards. Don't mention Preakness, lay out entire Belmont deal. They take it in. Pros. Solemn, sit chilly,
Oh Rafe why you ever mess with these boys? Thank you
very much Pablo, we'll handle it, that's all, that's enough.
Go out and win three.

Story breaks next day, no chance it won't, this not the
minors, this the big time baby. Plainclothes boys move in
114th and Third, knock nice and polite, then kick door in,
every piece ready. Nobody but his woman. Mr. Laguna?
Don't see him all week. Care if we look around? Why I care?
They look, tear it apart, put it back together, he's gone all
right. Plainclothes boys walk the neighborhood, very
proper, very polite. Everybody clams, but they pick up a
word here, a look there, bye-bye baby.

Catch up with him Oneonta, his Triple A moment of
glory. Picture in cuffs hits every paper NY State. Ramona
cloud nine. Knew he was good-for-nothing, saw it in his
eyes. Tell her do not want to discuss it, now, *ever*. Okay, still
no-good bum.

No-good bum don't give them a thing. Says took a
chance and lost, story of every gambler. Correction, says
one thing: should have known Pablo Diaz 100% honest
man. No-good bum don't say a word about Preakness, if he
does I'm dead, even though turned it down, must report
every nibble. Only talks Belmont, this n-g bum, don't even
hint who's into him. Maybe they hit him if he does, but
don't think that's the reason. Rafael a man, takes fall like
a man. Okay friend, I send your woman money, pay the
rent, look out for her, but I never talk to you long as I live.

Honest jock goes back to work. Round of applause first
time out. Loses on chalk, booed all way to jocks' room.
Back among friends.

Ramona so nice can hardly stand it. Tell her please go back to pain in the ass, face crinkles, never satisfied. Walk outside, circle my property. Shit, maybe she's right, story my life, never satisfied, more I get, more I want, 11 million this year, 15 next. Just the money? No, just *more.* Jump into Caddy, drive to 114th and Third. Nobody on street touch Caddy of Diaz. His woman lets me in. Sit in kitchen, drink beer, she sits in bedroom, watches TV. Stay three hours. When drive home all relaxed, beats goddam sleeping pill.

Next morning easy workout backstretch, Wineglo old sweet self. Sing nice as reward, walk him toward barn, hear my name, soft and low. Look to rail, almost fall off, catch self, walk him over. It's Ginny, tall, smooth, calm Ginny. Hop off Wineglo, turn him over to exercise boy, duck under rail.

Whathehell you doing here, Ginny?

Came up to give you some support.

I look around . . . Very nice of you baby, but don't need support.

Calm smile . . . Pablo, are you getting support from Ramona?

In a way . . . Yes . . . No . . .

No man is an island, Pablo.

Don't want to be an island, just a jock.

Calm smile, again . . . Staying at Garden City Hotel through Belmont. Pablo, I know what you've been going through.

Now my turn, calm smile . . . Nobody but Diaz knows that, Ginny.

The Garden City Hotel, Paul.

Shake my unsupported head . . . Ginny, you know my rule: Never do it on my own front lawn.

Rules are made to be broken, Paul. Are you happy with Ramona?

Whothehell knows?

Is she happy with you?

She better be. Ginny, go back to Florida. Please. Riding Calder middle of June, see you then.

Thank you, Pablo.

Meaning what?

Meaning thank you . . . Paul, if Ramona ever walks you know where I am.

Almost laugh, don't . . . Ginny, Ramona never walk, I'm her meal ticket.

Paul, if *you* ever walk you know where I am.

Have to give her my A-number-one stare, can't believe she talks like this, not with all her smarts and my training; finally have to spell it out: Ginny, you know damn well my religion forbids divorce.

Thinks about that, hard, face crinkles but this one never cries. All right, she says, I want to do some shopping in New York, but I'll be gone tomorrow, won't even stay for the race.

See you in June, I tell her as she walks away studying the grass.

Keep shaking my head. Head taking some beating this week. Look at classy, retreating frame, need this like horse with game leg. And Jewish broads supposed to be so smart.

Getting itchy, island fever. Inform Hy need something out of town, say Pennsylvania Derby Keystone end of May. Aye aye Cap'n. Lands Wotaguy, picturebook colt with one problem: specializes running just out of money. Tell Hy to mind store, have to solo, call Holly Carstairs, six-foot waitress Atlantic City, met her March after Cotillion. Take off in Mercedes, detour AC on way down, kick, coax, shove Wotaguy into show money, detour AC way back. Ready now, take on whole goddam world, including Belmont, Fat Bat, Cal Jones, odds.

Wineglo ships up fine, so does Mr. Pawkins. Tells me this horse given his life new meaning, true gift his age, you understand that Paul? Sure I understand, my hands, my head, my savvy *my* gift, why not a horse? Tell him do my best for you, Mr. Pawkins, answers haven't slightest doubt you will, my father never say that three million years. Even Tim very decent, give him high marks, has brought horse to this race lovely condition. Coat shines like Simoniz job, filled out, alert, strong. *Ready.* Work him myself: full of smooth juice, idles like my Mercedes. Tell Hymie, Hymie, can't win this horse, ship me back to Panama.

Come into race 3–1, good-looking odds. Fat Bat 8–5 to cop triple crown, makes sense unless you sit where I sit, atop lots of horse. Belmont packed, should be, 80,000, Ramona, Olga, Lorenzo guests Mr. Pawkins, Ginny home Bal Harbor, everything in place.

Move into gate quiet, easy, number six hole, eight-horse field. Fat Bat has rail, rail been gold today and Cal Jones dying prove west coast jocks for real, okay, be my guest. In gate use terrific will power, switch off waterfall of sound, silence, all is silence . . . CLANG, here we go baby.

Break good, 3rd, but take him back, out of trouble, tuck him in, close to rail. Up ahead Bat out fast, maybe too fast, this race good distance of ground, mile and a half, maybe too fast, maybe . .

Lay 5th for a mile, shake wrists, move him to outside, begin to pick up horses, Fat Bat starts to come back. Head of stretch and we're 2nd, resembles Preakness but got some room now, this is real race. Reach back, rap Wineglo once, twice, mean it, knows I mean it. Afterburners go off, *zooooom*. Catch Fat Bat, but he's tough, so is Cal, once again saddle to saddle, nose to nose. I'm hand-riding, so is he, don't hear the slash, smart move, no wasted motion, he's a pro. So is Diaz and this his turf. Go full quarter like that, a team, stride for stride, thrust for thrust, bob for bob, this is it, this is racing. Hit 16th pole still dead even, they don't give, we don't give, field somewhere back there, so long, good-bye. Whole world empty except for Bat, Cal, Wineglo, Diaz, no crowd, just us. Four hands lifting, pushing, nursing, pulling out that inch, reason we're here, the rest back there. Wire twelve strides away when feel it, the inch, two, a nose, a head, can't relax, more, more, my gift, God do this for nothing!

The end of silence. A *pistol* shot. Rafael's boys? Here? Can't be, too smart. Feel the sag, Christ know that sound now, heard it once before, Arlington, but not my horse . . . More sag, front left leg, the wire, half out of saddle, the wire, reach over, hold up his head, dead game, he's dead game. Hits wire on three legs, crumples, I'm out of saddle.

Can see it all so clear, slo-mo, just like whole world sees it, now, tonight, over and over, same as Rafe sees it in joint: Wineglo down, I'm sailing into space, like lazy cloud, roll over in air, slow, easy, Lorenzo love that, Fat Bat flows past, but the field pounding toward me, all in beautiful slo-mo. Start to float down now, will hit somewhere between neck and right shoulder, Wineglo gone, know it, please inject him fast, feel so bad for Mr. Pawkins, did I push too hard, too far? No, don't think it, don't feel it, no, my job, no . . . Track coming up to meet me, question is where? Cervical, dorsal, clavicle, head? My first time, so what, I win goddammit Rafe, I win. If I make it, tell Hy get off Calvin Klein ass, start working Travers Saratoga, maybe Scoliosis ready, earn your goddam money, here we come baby, oh please pray for me Ramona . . .

BAR BAR BAR

1

Fight, that's all they did lately and they had another one, a humdinger, and Howard Fu got on the bus absolutely determined to prove to Thomas that he wasn't sick in the head, that he knew *exactly* what he was doing, when it was time to stop he always stopped, and at his stage of the game why the hell did he have to explain anything to anybody, and that definitely included his son. That's when he saw her, with all the smoke coming out of his ears.

She was smiling out the window like the world was a gorgeous oyster, and she continued to smile (he would almost call it a grin, but a grin was something pasted on Mongolian idiots, and she was sure as shooting neither one), yes, to *smile* all the way through Queens, across the crazy quilt of Manhattan and even through the Lincoln Tunnel, about the dullest stretch of ground in America, unless in smiling you could hold back the mountain of water just waiting to pounce on frowners. When she continued like that through the turnpike, he really had to say something, polite, impolite, she had to know something he didn't know.

"Excuse me, but you certainly must like this trip."

She turned the Our-Gang comedy face to him (except it wasn't nasty, nor from that moment, whenever he saw it, even in his mind, could you ever call it nasty).

"Actually, it's my first time. That is, in forty years. I went to Atlantic City with my husband during the war."

The smile slid far back, then returned. "I understand it's changed."

"It's changed all right." He felt his neck (that's where he always got it, just like the expression, right in the neck), he felt it loosen up for the first time since he got up and knew he was in for it with Thomas. "Excuse me for saying so, but sometimes a person needs a little help if they don't know the ropes, don't be too bashful to ask."

"Oh," she said, "that's very nice, but I'm no gambler. I just like to look at other people and at things in general. Perhaps I'll walk out on the Steel Pier for old time's sake."

He didn't want to say it, but with Howard it was up front or nothing; besides, he didn't want to think of that smile disappearing in the morning fog.

"There's no Steel Pier no more." Say it and get it over with.

She did cut down a fraction of an inch, but she was game; it reminded him of Ruffian, and in his reminding, he begged her pardon for the comparison; also, of course, Ruffian was a filly; yet there was this thing about her, like a filly . . . "I should have known," she said gamely, "that's how it goes."

"That's how it goes, all right."

"Oh well, I'll settle for the boardwalk; there *must* be a boardwalk."

"Oh sure, there's a boardwalk," and he felt so good about letting her have her boardwalk that he repeated his offer.

"I'll send up a smoke signal if I need any help," she said with the game smile.

"You never know. I'll ride up to the rescue. With my white hat on. It'll say, 'Play at Claridge.' "

Not only did she smile, she giggled; Harriet never giggled in her entire life; to be more exact, when he cracked wise, she stared.

"Thank you," she said. "I'll keep my eyes peeled."

And that was that. Howard turned to his copy of *Winning Blackjack* and she looked out the window at the fascinating Jersey scenery and that's how they rode the rest of the way. The one time he looked up she was still doing it; anybody who could love Jersey must have had a permanent wave on her mouth. But it made him smile a little, too, and when they turned off onto the expressway, he began to feel the old surge of excitement.

It was some bomb. If they dropped it on Hong Kong it would wipe out the whole damn city.

He got this young black girl at Resorts who was glued to cards that topped him by one; she was scooping in his chips so monotonously that he was tempted to push them toward her as soon as she dealt him his nine, ten or picture. For that made it even worse: he was getting good cards; twice he hit twenty, twice she hit blackjack. By the time he slammed out to change his luck, he was down by seventy-five.

The salt air, plus the knowledge that win, lose or draw, the ocean would continue to do its number, calmed him down. He strolled into Bally's bound and determined to just worry about his own hand, the hell with the dealer.

She was in Bally's. Standing behind a red-faced lady with Popeye forearms who was working two bandits with so much alternate intensity that his shoulder practically ached. He cleared his throat, excused himself, and when the smiling face turned, asked her how she was doing.

"Hello there. Oh, I'm just watching. How about you?"

"Fair." (Never knock your luck; it could punish you even more.)

She turned to the red-faced lady, watched her snap down the arm, stare in disbelief.

"She's not breakin' the bank," Howard said.

Gazing once more, but not believing, the woman said over a chunky shoulder, "The bank hates me, I pumped both of these dry yesterday." She gave the arm a shot and it was no love tap and she said to the watching, smiling face, "They're all yours, the little rats," and stalked indignantly away.

"Wanna give it a try?" Howard said. "Sometimes, they give one person a hard time, then turn right around."

"Why should that be?"

"Search me, they got funny moods, I had a dog like that once. How about it, you got any quarters?" He copied her smile. "I don't wanna corrupt you."

"Oh it's too late for that," she said, not batting an eye. He noticed how smooth her blue-white hair was, not that it was plaster, but it stayed where it was supposed to stay. "I've never been lucky," she said while he was careful not to look at her hair. "I bought a sweepstakes ticket every year for thirty years and never won a dime."

Probably phonies, he thought, but never tell them. "Here, try a quarter," he said.

"Oh no, I have my own from the bus. Is this where you put it?"

"Correct. Right there."

She slipped in a quarter like it was made out of silk, pulled the arm very gently toward her and eased it back up; you would think it was sprained.

They gazed at two cherries, and five quarters tinkled out.

"Hey," Howard said, "I told you. Beginner's luck."

"It seemed so easy," she said, shaking her head and smiling at the cherries.

"Winning is so easy it can make you think you invented it," he said solemnly.

She nodded, she was a listener. "Well," she said, "as long as I'm Thomas Edison I'll put it all back."

"Well, it's your money, but why not keep three quarters and play two?"

"How about playing three?"

"Okay, that's a decent compromise."

She slid in the silk coins and caressed the arm down and then up. One bar revolved into the window and held, then another, then very promptly the third.

"Holy catfish," Howard said.

Even while she was asking, Are three bars good? the quarters jingled out; they were acting like they couldn't *wait* to be nice to her; quarters could do that with certain people . . .

"Three bars *must* be good," she said; he looked her over; yeah, she was sincere.

"They're excellent," he said. "You wanna pick up your loot or just leave it there and let it pile up?"

"Oh I'll leave it there, I'm not even playing on my money."

Pittsburgh Phil couldn't have said it better. She inserted three quarters with hands as soft as a great shortstop and did the nice easy pull. A 7 spun into place, then another; the third 7 didn't even hesitate. The quarters were Niagara Falls. Watching them with the smile, although she wasn't fainting dead away, she said, "I always did like that number."

"Lady," he said, "the main thing is the number likes *you*."

She turned full face while the last of the quarters tumbled out. "Well, at least for the moment, and you've been very helpful. I forgot my manners. I'm Carrie Greenbaum."

He shook the soft hand. "I know. I'm Howard Fu. You used to bring your husband's shirts to my place."

"Oh I'm sorry, sometimes I have a terrible memory." The smile flashed away, but then returned. "Of course. Your wife was . . . Oh dear . . ."

"Harriet. Practically the same name." And about the only thing that *was* the same . . . "Yeah," he said, "Mr. Greenbaum was a very nice man."

"Yes, he was." She smiled down at the pile of quarters. "He'd be so happy to see me winning . . ."

They had lunch in an indoor mall, which, he explained to her only when they were finished, used to be the site of the Steel Pier. She handled it fine. While she listened carefully, he explained that he was retired now, but between Atlantic City and Belmont he was busier than ever. He had always done a nice job of listening, so he nodded and said uh-huh as she told him she was also pretty busy, with Schools for Israel and fund-raisers like International Cheese Week and different Caribbean festivals at the temple. Still, there comes a time when you just want to be by yourself. He said, Pardon me, but that's the understatement of the week. Over ice cream she said, "There's a French laundry in your old place, isn't there?"

"Yeah," he said with a shrug. "But it's still mine. Up to a point. The rest of it belongs to my son."

"It must be gratifying to have your son follow you in your business . . ."

He looked into the clear eyes. "Not if he changes it to a French laundry."

She nodded very slowly as if memories were making her head pretty heavy. "That's what they call progress, isn't it?"

He nodded back, hard. "That's just what he told me. 'Progress, Pop.'"

After paying the check—she insisted on at least leaving the tip—he asked her if going into Playboy would bother her. She said, No, why should it? Well, my daughter-in-law gave me holy heck when she found out I went in there, so I never tell her anymore, but if *you* don't mind, I got very lucky there last week . . . She said, Sure, let's go.

He didn't get lucky. But Carrie did. She scooped out forty more dollars in quarters and her fingers got so grimy that he got her a couple of towelettes. What a nice touch, she said. With a smile that he had to work on he said, "I'm glad one of us could use them."

"Well, what's the verdict on Atlantic City?" he said as they sped through Jersey.

"I had a delightful day, Mr. Fu. I really did. And I appreciate your showing me what to do. I'm only sorry you didn't have a good day."

The funny thing was he didn't feel like bashing the window; his neck wasn't even stiff. "I got a philosophy. There's always *mañana* . . . How about it, Mrs. Green-baum?" He didn't translate, it wouldn't be necessary . . .

"Well why not?" No song and dance about plans or checking the calendar; just why not? And instead of beam-ing out at the miserable Jersey moonscape, she listened with complete attention as he explained the maddening intricacies of blackjack and the absolute treachery of rou-lette.

2

Howard left the house quickly the next morning without giving Thomas and Barbara time to do anything except exchange one of their fast glances. Carrie was right on the dot, waiting in front of the stationery store where they had bought the bus tickets the night before. Central America Night would just have to limp along without her.

"Did you tell them you weren't feeling so hot?"

"Oh no." The smile shut down a little. "I never do that. I told Jenny something else had come up." She brightened and so did he. He had goofed, but it was buried. Harriet would ride a goof like it was a six-day bike race.

When they got to Atlantic City they took the jitney to Harrah's, because, Howard explained, they had the same first initial. All right, she said.

As they walked into the clatter and bustle he asked her if she'd like to try a little blackjack. She could play it small because they kept the minimum down till later, but there was nothing like your own personal money to get in the swing. She didn't think so, she would just wander around until, and she smiled wide, she found a machine that had been absolutely miserable; they could meet right here for lunch. Okay, he said, don't forget to ask for towelettes. She liked that, he could tell. And she didn't wish him luck, she wished him *oceans* of luck.

He sat down at a table that was sending out letters of invitation, and decided to play it super-safe for a while to get a jump on recouping yesterday's disaster. He worked through two packs of cigarettes and managed to stay even, although a Puerto Rican dealer who kept rotating his shoulders like he was working out for the football season thought that tossing him an ace, a picture or a ten as a first card was a federal offense.

"How is it going?" the quiet voice asked.

He turned. A smile, but a concerned smile. "Hello, Bar Bar Bar. Hanging in, keepin' my nose above water. How about you?"

"Not so terrific today. I only won ten dollars."

"There's this thing about only winning ten dollars. It beats losing. Like that." He pointed at his stand-pat hand of fifteen and the PR dealer's twenty. "Okay." He picked up his remaining chips and stood. "Let's move to another table."

"Why?"

"Change my luck."

She turned as serious as he had seen her these two days. "I don't know anything about it, except what you told me, but if I may, why not just change your strategy? That way you don't give in to superstition."

He said gently, "People who play cards are superstitious."

"Maybe they shouldn't be."

He looked at the now-serious face and sat down and the dealer said, Are you in, sir? and he answered, Yeah, I'm in.

When his three cards added up to sixteen he turned to her. And she nodded, just like that. He scratched the top of the table softly and for a moment closed his eyes. He opened them to a four.

"Twenty should do it," she whispered.

He whispered back, "Don't hold your breath. This guy is from the FALN. He gets twenty-one. Watch."

He got nineteen.

"See?" she said, as he picked up two chips and fondled them, gazed at them. "Another thing . . ."

"I hear you."

"You should think more positively, if you don't mind the advice."

"I don't mind."

The dealer rotated his shoulders and began to shuffle. Howard said to her, forgetting the whisper, "Okay, from now on, I think positive."

"How will you do that?"

"How? Just think in this whole wide world *I* am the guy that has to win."

"I suppose that's all right . . ."

He swiveled around on his chair. "Hey, don't stop now."

"Well . . . I just think it's more productive if you take the personal aspect out of things . . ."

"How are you gonna take the personal aspect out of cards?"

"Well, *every*thing is personal when it comes to that."

The dealer rolled his neck and asked him to cut. "I never cut," he said and handed the yellow card to the man beside him who shrugged and cut. He said to her as the dealer packed the cards in the tray, "How would *you* think positive?"

"Oh . . . I don't know . . ."

"How, Carrie?"

The amazingly smooth forehead crinkled. "Let's see. All right, you asked for it." Crinkly smile. "When I was having my first child, Franklin, I was frightened to death. So I thought about Magellan."

"Magellan?"

"That's right. I decided if he could overcome a tremendous challenge, so could I."

The dealer cleared his throat. Howard swung back and pushed in two chips for ten dollars. Along came a four. He sighed, scratched, kept scratching and built up to eighteen. A sweep of the hand cut the dealer off. Over his shoulder he whispered, "What did he do?"

She bent close to his ear. "He sailed around the world for the first time. The *first* time. He was my greatest hero in high school."

"Was he a blackjack player?"

"Oh no. Well I don't think so." Without even looking he knew the smile was a honey. "Franklin," she whispered, "was beautiful and completely normal."

He looked down like he was studying his knees and closed his eyes. One thing he had was an imagination; Barbara had often said that, the last time when he told her Thomas would make a terrific Red Guard. Lonely, tough Magellan sailed through the casino on his way around the world: sharks, whales, cannibals, blowguns, headhunters, Amazons, Harriet's crazy family, seaweed, tidal waves, Jap savages, goof-off crew . . . He opened his eyes. The PR dealer's shoulders were quiet as a rock. His cards were so far over that Magellan was yelling with laughter all the way from Borneo.

They went to Atlantic City five times the next week. The third time she thought she would like to try a little roulette. He said you might as well see what a miserable game is all about. "I don't wanna tell you what to do, but you might want to take it easy and start out playing colors." She placed five chips on the black, but then at the last second murmured, "Oh heck," snatched them up and plunked them down on 13. He gazed in absolute agony but zipped up his twitching lip. The ball raced around the wheel like the nutty hamster he had bought Thomas at seven. It nestled in 13.

"Holy Moses," he croaked.

The croupier, a tall Irish girl, shoved stacks of chips at Carrie who smiled at them. She continued to look and smile while he kept his big mouth shut, but then she pushed one of the stacks back on the 13. There was a limit.

"Look," he said, "you're the Monte Carlo kid, but the odds against a number coming right back are out of sight."

"You think so?"

"It's my opinion, but ask anybody."

"What should I do?"

"Well . . . why not spread it around, you can even lap over two numbers, even four numbers . . ."

"But doesn't that reduce what I win?"

He had to look and nod at the Irish girl who grinned right back. "Yeah," he said, "but it covers you pretty good."

"But I have a hunch about the thirteen."

"Then take a piece of it."

The Irish girl got serious and hovered over her wheel. Carrie neatly placed her chips around the board, including a piece of the 13. The hamster started racing, the girl rasped out, "No more bets." He lit a cigarette.

The ball couldn't wait, it made a beeline for the 13 like Mom and Pop were waiting and he was late for dinner. Miss

Dublin placed her glass tube on the magic number, swept the table clean, pushed a small stack at Carrie and a young girl in shorts up to there.

"From now on," he said, "if I open the biggest mouth in America, don't listen."

"Oh I'll listen, all right." She patted his shoulder. "But I'll still play my hunch."

And that's what she did. The following week at Belmont. They were leaning on the rail at the paddock. She explained.

"You mean," Howard said, "if the horse *looks* at you while he's walkin' around?"

"That's right."

"If that's your hunch, that's your hunch . . ." He glanced at her sideways. "But isn't that very *personal?*"

"Well yes and no. Most of them ignore me. That's fine, that's their privilege. But if one *looks,* then it's between the two of us. It's a connection. He's telling me, let's trust each other, that's a *partner*ship."

"Suppose a few look?"

"I have a theory. One will always look harder."

"Okay." He leaned on the rail and looked hard; one horse glanced casually at him, but he was acting so rank it must have been a warning glance. He turned. "How about this? Take the second-hardest look and fill out an exacta?"

"What's that?"

"You pick one horse to win and one to come in second. Exactly."

"Howard, are you saying, pick one horse to lose?"

"Well, I'm saying come in *second* . . ."

"Second is losing," she said quietly.

"Forget it," he said. "Exactas drive you nuts."

That afternoon her system produced two winners. He hit no winners, but he did pick a forty-two-dollar exacta in the seventh. He didn't tell her.

When he walked into the house that night Thomas was waiting near the fireplace with his arms folded. Barbara was sitting near the TV with her legs crossed in that double-jointed way and she was holding on to one knee. He walked past them into the kitchen, pulled out a Budweiser, popped the ring and walked back. He sat down in his chair, drank and set the can down in an ashtray. Nobody asked him if he wanted a glass; they knew better.

"How'd you make out, Pop?" Thomas said.

"Not too bad." He took another drink.

"What's not too bad?"

"So-so."

"Did you break even?"

"Close."

"How close?"

He drank again. "Win some, lose some. Are you the district attorney?"

Barbara switched legs like greased lightning and grasped the other knee.

"No, Pop," Thomas said.

"So what's the third degree?"

Thomas leaned against the mantel, straightened out one of the smiling photos. "No third degree, Pop. We just don't want you to go overboard."

"I'm a big boy." He smiled at Barbara who shifted very slightly but didn't go into the crossover express.

"How did Mrs. Greenbaum make out, Pop?"

"Not too bad." He drank and set the can down with a clank.

"Want another one, Pop?"

"No thanks, I'll sit tight."

"Okay, Pop. Pop, can I ask you a question without you getting defensive?"

He looked them both over. "I don't know. Try. I don't promise a thing."

They finally did it, one of their speedball specials; they exchanged glances so fast a man with bad eyes would have missed it. Now that he had the signal, Thomas said, "Aren't you two getting very friendly?"

"What's it *to* you?"

"You said you wouldn't get defensive, Pop."

"I didn't say peanuts."

"Wait a minute, Thomas," Barbara said, still hanging on to her knee. "Dad, all we're trying to get at is the question of a possible relationship between you and Mrs. Greenbaum. That's all."

"That's a lot."

"Pop—"

"Please hold it, Thomas." She had a nice low voice when she was leaning on Thomas. "Dad, look at it this way. This neighborhood is very important to us. You and Tommy worked like dogs to get where we are. Dad, the neighborhood is an open book."

"Yeah?"

"You told me that yourself, remember?"

"I remember."

"Sure you do. Dad, a lot of people are very aware that you and Mrs. Greenbaum have been seen together."

"Is it in the paper?"

The speed-glance. "Dad, they are very aware of it."

"So what?"

"Simply the fact that you are *vul*nerable." She leaned

forward an inch and over the clenched legs looked at him with big, serious eyes.

"I'm doing okay," he said.

She sat back that inch. "Of course you are. And we want you to *continue* doing okay—"

"That's all we want, Pop. We don't—"

Her firm, slender hand was stopping traffic. "Hold it, please, Thomas." Thomas held it. "Dad, being vulnerable, you could get involved before you know it."

"We're not eloping tomorrow."

"Pop, why do you have to—"

"All right, Tom, all right. Thank you. Dad, we know you're not. That's not the point. The point is A leads to B, B leads to C. Before you know it . . ." Barbara always cocked her head to one side as she shrugged, like she was covering two bets. He flashed to Carrie and the calm, inner smile.

"She happens to be a very nice person," he said.

"Dad, I would not argue that statement for one second."

"Her husband was also a very nice person. Paid cash. On *time.*" He looked at Thomas. He looked at her.

"Of course, Dad. More than nice. Excellent. Both of them."

"He never gave me a hard time."

"I'm sure of that, Dad." Thomas let out a little sigh which she jumped right on top of. "Dad, they are and were excellent. No argument. But you are a very *special* man. You are *our* concern. We don't want to see that special man get hurt." She actually sat back, with her legs crossed. The room was quiet; if you have nothing to say, you have nothing to say. He and Barbara understood that. Not Thomas.

"Pop, do you bet for her?"

She stared at Thomas. Howard said, "What does that mean?"

"What I said. Do you bet for her with your money?"

"I cash in every T bill and give it to her. I also bet for Frank Sinatra."

"If that's supposed to be an answer, it's nowhere, Pop."

"Oh Tommy, Tommy—"

"Just take it easy. Whose father is he?" She folded into herself so hard she might never be able to get up. That was perfectly okay with Thomas. He nodded. "All right, Pop, you said you were a big boy so I'll give it to you straight. From one big boy to another—"

"Go on, big boy."

"All right. You know what they call them in Miami?"

"Dolphins?"

"Ha ha. Anthony Wang's kid goes to school down there, he'll tell you. *Barracudas.*"

"Is that a fact?"

"Call him up right now and ask him."

"Anthony's a jerk and his kid takes after his father."

"Did you ever?" But she was holding onto herself and Thomas had to keep charging on his own. He let go of the mantel. "All right, Pop. Ask somebody impartial. Ask Max. The druggist. You know what he'll tell you? *She* always wore the pants. *Always.*"

He swung casually to Barbara, the poor kid had made a very game effort. "Hey, impartial? Max made a play for her. She told me herself. And the woman is a hundred percent honest."

He kept looking at Barbara, which was driving Thomas up the wall, the way it used to with Harriet. "Yeah, Pop? Yeah? Well, I got news for you. Hot off the press. They *always* wear the pants."

She came suddenly out of her trance. "Oh Tom, must you always fall back on stereotypes? The next thing you'll—"

"I asked you once, whose father is he? It is time to call a spade a spade for crissake. I only want the man to put a zipper on his wallet as well as his pants."

"God, how gross. You are making this unbelievably gross."

"You think so? You think a man curls up and goes to sleep at his age? He's a strong man. He's a healthy man. You think *she's* packed it in? Max says she goes to Elizabeth Arden once a month. She knows—"

"Never mind what she knows. Will you come out of the gutter and discuss this rationally?"

"Are *you* naive? Do you realize how naive you are?"

But Howard was outside, walking fast and hard to Cuddahy's and thinking how quiet and peaceful and smiling she always was.

She wasn't smiling. She was sitting in the kitchen, listening to Franklin. Franklin across the table, softly, firmly: "It happens to be a fact, I couldn't possibly make it up. They'd rather gamble than eat."

"Maybe it's exaggerated a bit," she said gravely.

"Mama, they'll bet on the number of hairs on your head. Which floor the elevator will stop on. It's just a way of life. Did you ever hear of fan-tan?"

"No."

"It's a card game. It's practically baseball to them. The national pastime."

"He didn't make me do anything I didn't want to do, Franklin."

His mouth drooped for an instant but then straightened out. "I'm not trying to upset you," he said. "If it sounds that way, I'm sorry."

"I know, Franklin."

"I *want* you to enjoy yourself."

"I know."

"But in appropriate parameters."

She sat quietly and then reached over and touched his hand. "Don't aggravate so."

He patted her hand and said, "I'm Papa's son, I can't help it."

"He could have helped it and so can you. Franklin, you have no idea how beautiful the horses are."

He looked around the room before answering. "He never went to the track in his *entire* life."

"Neither of us did."

"May I ask a question?"

"Of course."

"What would he say?"

"I really don't know."

"Do you think he would say throw your money away on fan-tan?"

"I doubt it, Franklin."

"I'm going to tell you something. I never mentioned this because I never like to bring my work home. Last year we had to let a top man go after just six months. Number three in his class. Law Review. He just couldn't stop. It got into his blood. Like hepatitis."

"I promise I'll be careful."

He got up and walked to the refrigerator and came back and sat down. When he did that . . . "Mama, I'm going to do something I really don't want to do. It has never been my style, but I couldn't look at myself in the morning if I didn't do this. Mama, I do not want you to go to Atlantic

City with that man again. If you enjoy it that much and feel it's important to you, it's *that* important to you, then *I'll* take you. I'll call in sick. That includes Belmont."

She covered his hand and said gently, "Thank you, that's very sweet. But it will have to be the week after next. Next week we're going to Las Vegas."

They spent four days at Caesar's Palace and she broke even while Howard lost a hundred, which he said was breaking even for him. The day after they flew back, since the horses had left Belmont, they drove up to Saratoga. They stayed in a motel outside of Glens Falls because it was so spur-of-the-moment, but they caught all nine races every day for six days, including the Sanford, where, he told her, Man o' War had been upset by Upset. And when they drove home, no one said anything to anyone. The next day, however, Howard called and asked if she could come over, it was fairly important, but take your time.

He met her at the door and they walked inside and there was Franklin, standing in the center of the living room having one of his earnest conversations with two people. They could only be Thomas and Barbara, no need even for an introduction. Although she got one, quickly from Howard, earnestly from Franklin. Along with, "Here, sit down, Mama."

He pointed to a lovely recliner and she took it, although she didn't recline. Howard pulled a hard chair alongside the recliner and sat down rather hard. Crossed his arms. Thomas and Barbara remained seated on a convertible sofa. Franklin slouched in the middle of everybody with his hands in his pockets. That meant he was chairman.

"Mama," he began, "and Mr. Fu," and he smiled at

Howard who didn't smile back, "the three of us have taken the liberty of chatting together and we all agree that the time has come to openly discuss this situation." Thomas opened his mouth, but Barbara squeezed his arm and he shut it. "We," Franklin said, "that is, we three, really think the whole thing should be ventilated."

"All right," she said.

Scrunching his eyes together, which showed he was thinking hard, Franklin said, "Mama—and Mr. Fu—we could be wrong, although we don't think we are, but we believe a situation like this can only grow more complicated. Do you see our point?"

"I see it."

"Going to Atlantic City, or even to the track on a single-day basis is one thing. Going on extended trips is another. It puts the whole thing on a different plane. You see my point?"

"Yes, I do see it."

With his arms still folded, Howard said, "We stayed in separate rooms."

"That rates a medal, Pop," Thomas said before Barbara's hand could shoot out. Howard shrugged.

"Thomas," Franklin said, "we *did* agree?" Thomas sat back, Barbara nodded. Franklin scrunched his eyes some more (he'd had terrible crow's feet at seventeen) and said, "Mama—and Mr. Fu . . . Howard . . . it's quite obvious we cannot stop two adults from seeing each other. Even if we wanted to. The question is, where do we go from here?"

She looked at Howard and he gave her a quick nod. "We *had* thought of going to Reno," she said.

Thomas rolled his eyes around the room while Barbara clutched tightly. Franklin unscrunched his eyes. He even smiled. "In the old days, Mama," and he looked at everybody, "folks . . . in the old days they said so-and-so went to Reno to get Reno-vated. Meaning divorced."

"They had casinos before Vegas," Howard said.

"Really? I guess that took the sting out of Reno-vating." He walked to Carrie and peered down. "Mama, how involved are you?"

She felt Howard's eyes. "We enjoy going out," she said.

He took his hands out of his pockets. "Quite frankly, Mama, are you talking marriage?"

She turned toward Howard's eyes and Franklin's voice followed: "Mother, you have always been the most honest person I have ever known. . . . Are you?"

"No."

She looked up at Franklin who gazed at her for a moment, then stepped back and nodded at Thomas and Barbara. So fast that it could easily have been missed, they nodded back.

Howard was out of his chair like he had just hit a 50–1 shot, and everyone jumped, and he was pumping Franklin's hand and saying, "Mr. Greenbaum, you're okay, you're terrific," and he practically yanked Carrie to her feet and he said, "Holy smokes, Carrie, how about it, you wanna get married?"

Into the deathly silence she said, "Why yes, Howard."

Stephen Greenbaum flew in from Fort Worth. He and Franklin had a meeting with Rabbi Weiss which was not too productive because the Rabbi kept saying why not look at the bright side, but never described the bright side. Meanwhile, Thomas and Barbara talked to Father Villensky, but Father Villensky hadn't seen Howard in twelve years and strongly suspected he'd gone back to Confucianism, in which case he wouldn't touch it with a ten-foot pole, this wasn't the old days, you know.

After a week of on-and-off discussions with her sons, Carrie told them, "We've decided to get married in Reno."

Franklin, who was looking very tired, said, "I don't know what's happening around here."

"It will be the best thing," she said, patting his hand.

"Do they have a temple in Reno?" he said, holding the bridge of his nose.

"How about going on TV in a casino?" Stephen said. Franklin stared at him.

"We'll go to a justice of the peace," she said.

"How about a little girl playing the wedding march on a baby grand?" Stephen said, and as Franklin stared, he murmured, "Jesus Christ."

"That's enough, Milton Berle," she said.

"You know me, Ma," Stephen said. "I'm harmless."

"I know you."

Franklin let go of his nose. "What about afterwards, Mama?"

"Afterwards we'll come back and set up housekeeping."

"Where?"

"Howard's cousin is in a new building near Mulberry Street. He can get us in."

"You're going to live in Chinatown?"

"It's a lovely building. It has balconies."

"Balconies? In Chinatown? Jesus Christ."

"Just keep calm, Franklin."

"Did you hear that, Steve?"

"I heard." He glanced at Carrie. "Ma's right, take it easy, Frankie. Ma, let me talk to him."

She got up. "All right, I'll have some Sanka, then I'm going to take a bath and go to bed. It's enough for one night. I'm getting very tired of this, Steve."

"I know, Ma. You go inside and make your Sanka. I'll talk to him."

"No comedy, Steve."

"No, Ma, I promise."

She walked into the kitchen without another word.

After a long time, with his head nodding, as if he were back in temple as a little boy, Franklin said, "My one wish, which has obviously been granted, is that there's no heaven."

Stephen nodded too, but hard, twice. "So he can't look down and see, right?"

"You got it," Franklin said. "He wasn't the world's greatest father, but he didn't deserve this."

"Frankie, maybe it's not so terrible."

Franklin looked at his brother; he was too tired to scrunch his eyes. "You sound like Weiss."

"Don't be a goddam idiot, Frankie."

"Thanks very much for your support. I knew I could count on you. Steve, I realize you're the original freethinker and Tommy Manville was your role model, but I'll tell you what I think: I think it is *obscene.*"

"She won't get pregnant, Frankie."

"Will you please cut that out? With my luck, there *is* a heaven, and he *is* looking down."

"All right, Frankie, you know what he would say? I'll tell you *exactly* what he would say. You want them to live in Jamaica Estates?"

Stephen flew back to Fort Worth the next day, but left a note saying please call when you hit Reno, I'll jump up and buy you a wedding brunch and cheer for you at the wheel of fortune. She called him that night and said she just might take him up.

They were to leave on a Wednesday. On Tuesday afternoon the phone rang in Franklin's office. Since Martha was on her coffee break, he picked it up and barked, "Yeah, Greenbaum."

"This is Thomas Fu."

"Oh. Yes. Look, Thomas, if you don't mind a little advice, let's leave it alone. Once the troops go in on D day, you can't pull them back."

"I don't know about D day, but you can relax."

He looked into the phone, shifted it to the other ear. "Your priest got to him?"

"No way. He's in the hospital."

". . . Hospital?"

"He got up during the night to go to the bathroom and keeled over. We heard this noise, it sounded like the ceiling came down. We found him on the floor."

". . . Yes?"

"We called 911, they're really on the ball, the ambulance got here in nothing flat."

"Yes?"

"The medics were right on the ball, I told them I'd write a letter for their file. It gives you some hope the city's coming back."

"What happened at the hospital, Thomas?"

"They admitted him immediately. One look, he was in, no red tape."

"Yes? And?"

"They think it's a stroke."

"Christ."

"They're not a hundred percent sure yet, but they're pretty sure. His right side is paralyzed and he can't talk."

". . . What's the prognosis?"

"They don't know yet, but it doesn't look too good. He's a tough old bird, but like they said, at his age you never know. Your mother is with him. It's funny, you never know, do you?"

"My mother?"

"She came right over as soon as I called. We figured it was the right thing to do."

"Of course. Where is he?"

"Saint Catherine. They've been great, they run a real tight ship."

"Yes, I've heard . . ."

"I don't want to jump the gun, but I think I better start looking around for a home."

"That's an arm and a leg, Thomas."

"You're telling me? That's why I better start looking."

"Do you have power of attorney?"

"Thank goodness. My cousin straightened me out on that when I took over the business."

"If you need any help . . . ?"

"Thanks, but Wallace is excellent. Well, it's crazy, but you can relax now."

"So can you, Thomas."

"Not exactly. I got the home to worry about."

"Of course. Can I visit?"

"You better call the hospital. And be prepared, I don't think he'll know you."

"Well . . . I'll give it a try."

"Okay, but be prepared, I'm not even sure he knows *me.*"

"Thank you, Thomas. I appreciate your calling."

"Sure. Isn't this a kick in the pants?"

He rang off and immediately called Forth Worth. Then the hospital.

The lady at the desk asked his name and then walked to a phone and dialed and said, "He's here." She asked him to please wait. A tiny doctor from somewhere in East Asia came striding down the corridor, shook his hand and said he was very pleased he had come, please, let's talk over here. He took Franklin's arm and steered him to a leather sofa in the patient-lounge area. He briskly gave Franklin his name: it came out like Vanloppis or Tanlappis; Franklin called him sir. Sitting down, he looked like a high school boy.

"I'm the attending physician for Mr. Fu and I understand you are very interested in him, therefore I felt I should talk to you."

"That's very decent of you, sir. How . . . bad is it?"

"We are not sure yet. I have directed more tests. I prefer not to say too much until the results come back."

"Of course. Perhaps I should come back when you have a handle on things."

He shook his head briskly; he did everything like a brisk little brown bird. "Makes little difference. As long as you do not have a cold or other infection, it's all right. Infections are terrible."

"I understand, sir. I don't have a cold."

"Good. I really want to talk to you about your mother. Mrs. Carrie Greenbaum. She *is* your mother?"

"Yes, sir . . . Did she take it very hard?"

He nodded briskly. "I would say yes."

". . . I was afraid of that . . . Is she still here?"

Brisk nod. "She is in a room on his floor."

"Sir?"

He leaned forward and his white coat drooped on the floor. He said, "Your mother came to visit. The nurse on duty, a very competent person, came in to check on Mr. Fu as directed. She found your mother sitting very stiffly beside him and as a competent nurse she became alarmed. She spoke in quite a loud tone to your mother but received no response . . ."

"I don't quite follow you, sir."

"Please bear with me and all will become clear. The nurse immediately called me and I immediately came and examined your mother." Three brisk nods. "There was no response. She was unable to move at that point. We took the liberty of examining her purse, for this appeared to be an emergency. We discovered your name and number and I directed the nurse to call you." Nod, nod. "But of course you were on your way here. Fortunately, we had a bed. I took it on myself to place your mother in this hospital. You may wish to move her. Frankly, the professional care of this institution is the equal of those in Manhattan or even London. But that is up to you."

"I . . . this place is fine . . . I'm sure . ."

"You can believe me. You will have to fill out some forms at the desk. You can do it later."

"I appreciate that . . . Sir, did she . . . have a . . . stroke?"

"Frankly, I am not sure. My own opinion is this: It is not an organic condition. As far as I can now see."

". . . What does that mean, sir?"

"I would say it is an hysterical reaction."

"Sir, I don't want to sound as though I'm questioning anything you've said, but I should tell you that my mother is an *amazingly* calm person . . ."

Sure enough, a brisk smile. "It is a question of semantics. We say hysterical in the sense of a *functional* response. Let me see . . . a state of mind?"

"You mean a shock?"

Brisk shrug. "Good enough. A shock."

"Can I see her?"

"No reason why you cannot. 303. Mr. Fu is in 307. Perhaps seeing you will help. Notify the nurse instantly if something extraordinary occurs. You can fill out the forms later." He held out his hand and Franklin took it and they shook briskly. "Good luck, Mr. Greenbaum, we try with equal force, no matter the age, I have seen this condition a number of times." And he was striding briskly down the hall with his coat flapping around his ankles.

She was staring at the ceiling when he walked in, but as he approached the bed her eyes shifted and fixed on his face. The pupils were very dilated. He didn't sit down.

"Mama, do you know who I am?"

She looked up at him.

"It's Franklin." He wanted to touch her hand but he didn't. "You can fight this," he said.

She looked up at him.

"I feel terrible about . . . the whole . . . thing. Everybody feels terrible . . . But you can't let it lick you . . ."

She looked up at him.

He wanted to touch her forehead, check for fever. "We're with you all the way . . . I called Steve, he's flying back . . ."

She looked up at him.

"Mama, that doctor looks like a very good man. They work extra hard . . . You have terrific willpower, next to you we were all cream puffs . . . Why don't you try, Mama?"

She looked up at him.

"Mama, I have a client whose brother-in-law is a top man at Rusk. I'll talk to him. This will work out, you'll see. But you have to cooperate."

She continued to look at him and he wanted to bend down and kiss her, but he turned and walked out and downstairs he filled out the forms. Then he went back to the office.

It was close to midnight when Carrie opened her eyes. She waited for a bit, then very carefully reached over and bent the gooseneck lamp close to the table and turned it on. She drew her legs up and out of the covers. Slowly, she lowered the guard rail. She swung around and located her slippers, then turned off the lamp. She sat there for a moment. Now she eased into the slippers, walked toward the crack of light under the door. She reached the door, opened it, looked out. The nurse at the end of the corridor was sipping from a cup and looking at a magazine.

She stepped out, closed her door, walked swiftly the few yards, keeping close to the wall. She opened the door to 307 and slipped inside. She closed the door, waited until she could see and then walked to his table and turned on the gooseneck and bent it far down. She lowered the guard rail and sat on his bed beside him.

His eyes fluttered open. He stared up at her. She leaned close to him and whispered, "It's all right, it's me, Howard, don't be afraid . . . Howard? Blink once if you can hear me. Go on."

He blinked once.

"Very good. Now, I want you to pay careful attention. Listen carefully now. You have a blackjack hand of fifteen. You have decided to play it very bold. Howard, either you want a card or you don't. Remember, *bold.* All right now, blink once if you want a card for bold, blink twice if you just want to stand pat."

He stared up at her.

"Come on now. Once for bold, twice to stand pat."

He blinked once.

"*That's* a good boy. And you got a six for twenty-one! Very good. Now Howard, listen to this. If you get one bar when you play the bandit, how many more do you need to win? Come on, Howard, how many? Blink the number."

He blinked once. Again.

"That's *excellent.* You're doing beautifully. You see how we'll work together? No matter what? Blink once if you understand that."

He blinked once.

"Beautiful." She bent closer. "Don't worry and don't be afraid; they'll never trick me into leaving you. All right? Blink once if it's all right."

He blinked once.

"That's my Howard. All right, let's try another. You're at the roulette wheel. You have all your chips on thirteen. The wheel is spinning. Now Howard, you can be very personal and just think about yourself, or you can think about

Magellan the way I showed you. Now concentrate. Blink once if you're going to worry about yourself. Blink *twice* if you're going to reach out and go for Magellan. I'm right here, Howard, I'll *always* be here. Come on, is it going to be Magellan, Howard?"

He stared at her. A small round tear began to blossom at the inner corner of each eye.

OPERATION
BUENA VISTA

The proud red glow was gone and for a terrible moment Henry thought the gateway to the West had been wiped out in the night. Then he reached for his field glasses, sighted along his secret tunnel off 95th Street, out over the river, over the folded layers of laminated shale (known to the dumber guys as the Palisades) and closed his eyes. In his head he filled in the space above the water. When he was good and ready, he drove his eyelids apart and stared with all the stored-up power of history, geography and manifest destiny. *Whew.* The old combo had worked again; against the new day the dim, spidery grayness hung limp but unmistakable: ALCOA. *Whew.* You never knew what you would wake up and not find these days. Satisfied, he slid his glasses into the case, threaded his way over Ezzard (still smiling over his latest hookshot) and slipped into the bathroom. As he brushed and flossed his teeth, he could see out the window, near the gateway, another corner of the western plain, where brave young Hamilton, bright as ALCOA at midnight, had been lured to that fatal shootout. Poor sonuvabitch. If only a guy like Henry had been around to clue Ham, Aaron the Burro would have got his shit kicked out all the way from Weehawken to Princeton Township. A mouthful of toothpaste water finished old Aaron and spun him down the drain like a nothing cockroach. Henry walked back to his room and whipped into his A.M. assembly clothes: white shirt, red tie and navy blue jacket. As he wound up the double windsor knot, he previewed the day, bigger than any damn assembly with its General Electric crap or dumbass trampolines. Finishing with a quick scuff of each shoe against his trousers, he walked into the kitchen and sat down before the piled-up books. The all-important permission slip lay in his history, next to the page about the stupidass Hessians. He drew it out and curled it up just a little, figuring on a quick shove and pullaway between toast and coffee and a playitdumb request. Not that he anticipated trouble, but with the old Spraygun, you never knew. Today *could* be his day; then again, ol Spray might wanna preach. Maybe the slope of the curve, which hadn't been preached since he got 82 in first quarter arithmetic. ("Why you a 98, son. Goddam that curve got to slope *up.*") He unfolded the slip and focused on the Princeton part, which was the *real* slope, up the hill from the Delaware, out past the ALCOA gate and laminated shale, far beyond any goddam 98 in arithmetic.

"Whachou got there?"

Uh oh, ol Spray had beat him to the draw, he slapped leather fast that ol Gun.

"Jus a little permission slip," he said absently, smiling at his mother, whose back was turned.

"What kinda permission slip?"

He caught Ezz sliding into a chair, ears and eyes working overtime.

"Oh nothin much."

"Henry, your father is asking you a question. Now you just answer his question."

ALCOA was receding into the gathering sunlight and Weehawken wasn't helping much. "Well," he said, "it's jus a little field trip we goin on."

Ezz gave him the suckin eggs and he knew all at once the Gunner had a rough day. Sure enough . . .

"Complaints all goddam day. Now he tells me jus another field trip," his father said, abusing his toast. The room echoed to chewing and gulping.

Finally, "It's only to Princeton," Henry said. He dug into his Shredded Wheat and swallowed. "We gonna see where Washington crossed the Delaware, and Nassau Hall, which useta be the Capitol, and we gonna see a baseball practice."

"Who's gonna pay?"

"Well I thought . . ."

"Samuel," his mother said, "I can give him the money. It sounds like a nice trip."

"Yeah, it sounds very nice." The coffee flew down his father's throat. Ezz giggled. Damn Ezz, he get his ass kicked later on. "Henry," his father said, wiping his mouth. "I'm gonna say somethin to you you ain't gonna like. You might not even understand it. But I'm gonna say it. I don't want you goin on no more trips."

"Well I got the money, Dad. I got enough. So if you jus sign . . ."

"No, Henry. It ain't the money." His father tipped his chair back. Damn, the slope of the curve. "Like I said, maybe you won't get this. I don't want you goin to no Princeton."

"Why not?"

"I tell you why." The voice was nice and quiet, like it was about to say, Step back please? Instead it said funny things. Awful funny. Like it said, "Well, that's no place for you; it's a fool place."

"How come?" His mother's eyes were asking too.

"Henry," the quiet voice said, "you foolin around too much with this stuff. Now you goin to junior high in a few months an you gotta start wakin up. Jus tell me this, what's wrong with New York City?"

"Nothin wrong with New York City. Why can't I go to Princeton?"

"Because, Henry, you ain't got *nothin there.*"

"What? What kinda nothin?"

"Henry, I know them places over the river. I worked four years in Tom's Ford. Hell, Tom's Cabin."

"Now Samuel," his mother said, "it's only a trip."

"It's *not* only a trip. Now it's time this boy woke up with all his history an geography an dreamin. Right now, dammit. All his goddam history and geography is right here. Henry, boy, this town is *yours*. Why there's more colored people in New York than any city in the world."

"There's colored people in Princeton. They go back to the revolution."

"Hell, they're poormouth, Henry; they're pussyfooters."

Somethin funny was goin on, very funny and Ezz was a part of it, those eyes and ears buggin and flappin. Whatinhell was such a big deal about a field trip . . . ?

"Henry," his father said, leaning in, his face looking gray and very tired. "Listen, you got to learn what's what."

Henry walked slowly down Columbus Avenue, keeping a careful block behind Barbara Jones and Joseph O'Loughlin. At 83rd Street Isolina, Katherine and Leandre swung out. Isolina looked back and waved and hesitated. Without even trying, Henry turned to the Food Fair window and suddenly became fascinated with Del Monte. He studied diced pineapple for five minutes and when he sneaked a look back, they were turning in for the school, Isolina kicking her skirt up and looking straight ahead. Sighing, he stepped away from Del Monte and started downtown, feeling in his inside pocket the empty last line of the permission slip that assigned him to charades, gym and study, while Isey flounced all over the turning point of the revolution. For a moment he thought of scribbling Samuel Strothers,

Joseph's old report card bit, and charging the entire day to the Gunner's conscience. Serve him goddam right, treating his own kid like a shitass Benedic Arnold. Shoot man, he scolded, that ain't no way, walking around Princeton with a goddam forgery in your pocket like a lousy British agent. He took out the slip and tore it up and jammed the pieces into a wire can that asked for a clean city. If only he could stuff the Gunner's words into that can, have them carted out to the goddam incinerator and burned to nothin. He sighed. Shit, why he have to say those crazy things anyway? Crazy goddam things. And Mama, like a goddam echo sayin listen to your father now, he been through it all. Ezz givin him the old cream eyes. Shit. A mailbox offered leaning space and he draped over it and twisted back for a view of the project. Fourteenth floor, corner. Still up there beatin their gums. He straightened up, shook his head and started down again. Crazy old Gunner. You could turn off the regular crap like the chemistry and lectricity, and the goddam slope of the curve. Yeah you could flick off that jazz with one ear; but that other crap, *that* kept coming, like the fuckin British up Bunker Hill . . . "Listen, Hank, go down the subway any day and night, what you see? Hah? Black faces. That's what. An what I see every day in the bus? More them faces. Hank they *used* to be white. No more. Understand, Hank?" . . . Big fuckin deal. And he kept comin, just kept chargin . . . "Henry, sometime I wait awhile before I give out the change. Jus a little. I give them white hands a fumble an a little hesitation an they *take* it." I hang your ass up with the company, he thought, if you fumble me . . . "An Henry, I know places like that Princeton. You *ever* see a colored boy on their football team? You think you see one at baseball practice today?" Well, no colored boy make the team, that's all . . . "Well Henry, jus look at CCNY, boy that whole *school* is dark. An Henry they got the best chemistry and lectricity courses in the whole country . . ." Yeah, that's the ol Gunner, the ol crap, the easy stuff, jus reach up and turn it off; and with it finally, with a deep breath, the new jazz hangin on to the lousy slope. The Spraygun was silent at last, only the face kept flappin. Shoot. He erased the face like it was a blackboard, with hard, wide strokes. Shoot.

He turned into 68th Street and saw the lineup of buses. The classes coming down, ragged double file, with Mr. Wunderson and Miss Debono. Assembly clothing and lunch bags, then Joseph and Isolina. Isolina hanging back and jerking her arms at him, that hot temper commanding him to run. Poor hot Isey. Today she'd have to get her geography from Joseph and dumb Joseph thinks Europe in South America. It all began to pile up and spill over, up into his goddam eyeballs—Isey and Joseph and the Gun ridin up his friggin slope, fumblin with his changemaker, the yellow buses gettin all goddam misty. Disgusted, he about-faced and walked away from the school.

The great circle route started at 72nd and Riverside. That was the kickoff point, right at the major confluence of the Ohio and the Monongahela. That's where he took his first bearing, gazing through the binocs straight across river to where Hamilton got the business. Right next to Colonel Stevens' Castle, top of the great hill that guarded the South Passage inland. Yeah man, them buses would swoop out the tunnel with them dopes munchin their Yankee Doodles and nobody even *dream* whatehell was doin up above in Weehawken Heights or on the Hoboken Plain. How could they? Joseph was no Meriwether Lewis and Isey no goddam Sacajawea. Sheeit.

He moved up the Drive, glasses at the ready, senses

honed for action any place in the territory. White marble Soldiers and Sailors at 89th with those fat ol guns, hunched over and miserable. Casing his glasses, he mounted gently and sat astride one of the sad little guys and patted the round belly. Hell, he told all the busloads and his father and Ezz, you be miserable too if you plucked out of Fort Necessity and plopped down here with all the rubberass babies slobberin over you, and all sealed up inside so you're a goddam joke. He stroked the tough old pitted hide and slid off and walked up Riverside, feeling real bad for lost smoke and flame and glory. Plenty of head shakes.

At 106th Street, he came to conniving Franny Sigel, staring over the water. He shinnied up the prancing horse and sat alongside Franny and gazed out with him. Everbody who knows somethin lookin out, he thought, everbody, out over the plains and basins and open pits. His sightline cut the SPRY sign. Smiling, he looked pityingly down at the four kids playin Elliott Ness. Poor bastids, thinkin SPRY for fryin like the dumb sign say. Leaning into Franny's ear, he whispered the SPRY words they shared for today: Silver City, Pawnee, Rosebud, Yellow Medicine. He rubbed Sigel's ageless, all-seeing eyes that gathered in the magnificence of SPRY country. Okay Franny baby, you old pisscutter, Henry Strothers check it all out for you someday. Right where you lookin.

He leaped down, told one of the dumb kids watch how you playin, this govment propety man, and walked back to the west (the important) side of the Drive and continued uptown. Up past Fort Lee that guarded the North Passage, and Palisades Park that looped so playfully over the shale. Up to 178th Street where at three o'clock he stopped for a Pep and a Twinsicle.

Having made reconnaissance and taken refreshment, Captain H. A. Strothers, Third Platoon, Fourth Regiment,

Rogers' Rifles, climbed down the embankment and out onto the thin spit of land next to the lighthouse and stared up and out at the challenge and invitation of the Northwest Passage. The great, spidery link arched protectively over his head; the sun was warm; he was pleased with the whole operation and he was ready.

He sat on a flat rock and pulled out the latest communiqué. Spreading it carefully out, he hunched over and for the fiftieth time absorbed the message.

May 3
54 Lake Street
Duluth, Minn.

Dear Henry,

I got your last letter okay. It was fine, a real good letter. Well I'm sitting down and replying just before supper and I'll tell you the stuff just like you asked me to. Well from up here next to the Skyline Drive I'm looking down on Superior and I can see three big wheat barges. One is pumping wheat. The lights are coming on and the people on the breakwater pier are walking around and one guy is fishing. Hey right now the rising bridge is rising! Henry, did you know its the highest rising bridge in the world? Well it is. I can still see Wisconsin though not to good. Well thats the scene from here. Now as to what I've been doing, yesterday Dad took me up to Mesabi and let me go down the pits with him. Boy was I scared. But after a while you get used to it and its a lot of fun. Henry, did you know its the largest open pit in the world? Well it is. As to next week, we're going up to Indian Point next to Canada to look over the old trading post. Next month our class is taking a trip to the Black Hills and I'll send you some dirt from the Big Horn. Thanks for your dirt from Washington Heights. Well Henry, thats about all from here. I have to get ready for supper. Write soon and don't forget about this summer.

Your friend,
Lance Olsen

P.S. *Maybe this year the Twins will knock off the Yanks?!*

He stroked it and read it and re-read it. Then he looked up and followed the arch of the bridge to where it hooked onto the mainland. Downstream from the hookup, the great sign, thick and silvery in the daylight, stood up and pointed the way to the biggest open range, the highest rising bridge, the largest open pit in the world.

After supper his father came into his room and gave him a present, "Math Puzzles for Young Scientists," and while Ezz leaned sideways over his spelling and slanted his eyes, the inevitable reverse talking began.

"Henry, I didn't mean to jump down your throat this mornin."

"That's all right."

"No it ain't. I want to explain things better. I don't want to wup you into understandin."

"It's okay. Forget it."

"It ain't okay. I wanna explain."

"Ezz gonna listen?"

"Yes he is. This important for both of you."

Eveready Ezz closed his looseleaf and swung around like he was on a pivot. With a deep sigh, Henry bent the gooseneck over his relief map. "Well Daddy," he said, "it was jus a permission slip."

"That ain't the *point*. It's the whole way you goin, Henry."

"Which way I'm goin?"

"All this stuff, the maps, the way you thinkin. Henry it jus ain't good for you. Believe me."

"Why?"

"Why, why. Ever since you a baby. Allus why. Ezz don't ask why. Ezz *trust* in me."

"Ezz a jerk."

The soft, high moan started (naturally), only to be snuffed out by his father's upraised arm. "Okay okay Ezzard, I'm talkin. Henry *teasin* you. Can't you see that?" Mr. Strothers rubbed his face. "Henry," he said, "you so smart. Why can't you use your brains an pull *with* me. It's for *your* good. Henry, I don't wanna see you hurt."

"How I'm gonna be hurt?"

"Okay son, okay, I tell you how. Henry, you know who you named after? You named after Henry *Arm*strong. Hammerin Henry Armstrong."

"Who he?"

"See, you don't know everything. He jus the greates fighter ever lived, pound for pound, that's all. Oh man, he was fast and tough. He murdered Barney Ross."

"I thought Joe Louis the best."

"Shoot. Only cause he was a heavyweight. Armstrong was a welter and he beat em all. Even middleweights. Till the end."

"What happen then?"

"Hell, they used him up. Like an old rag. Made a punchin bag outta him, till he was nothin. Jus like they did Ezzard Charles."

"That who Ezzard is?"

"That's right. *He* was a heavyweight, but move like a cat. Smooth as silk. He *beat* Louis. An Henry, he didn't even *like* fightin. Then they squeezed him down to nothin. Like Armstrong. Well you an Ezz, you gonna *become* somethin, not old dried-up rags. You gonna carry on. All the way. You gonna make it for them cause you got the chance they never had. You fellas got it all; you gonna hammer; you gonna be smooth; you gonna use your opportunities an you won't get beat the way they got beat. See?"

"I'm usin my opportunities, Daddy."

"No you ain't. That's what I'm tellin you. Why I sweat overtime an your mother do cleanin? Jus for you fellas. So we move down from Harlem and do right for you. An what do *you* wanna do? All you wanna do is cowboys and Indians. Shoot."

Goddam Ezz, he think he boppin Joe Louis all over again, sittin up straight, kissin ass all over the room. Man, awful hard talkin to the Gun when his voice crack and he shoot spit; but a guy got to protect his country.

"There's *some* cowboys an Indians, Daddy, but mostly they're in history." Maybe a few facts. Trouble with the Gun was he never have any facts. "Daddy, you know the Mississippi Missouri the longest river in the world. It's called the father of waters."

The voice cracked higher. "It's mud, Henry. Mud. I seen it. Not in some damn book either. It was a *slave* river. Still is. Henry, I tell you somethin, you big enough. When I was in the army, stationed near Vicksburg—one of your goddam history towns—I couldn't even get a sandwich in a diner. An right in there, proud as punch, a damn German prisner war was feedin his face together with a dozen MPs. That's your father of waters."

Ezz was rocking with joy; his father just kept on hammering.

"Henry, here is where you got it. Here. This the greatest city in the whole world."

"Yeah, it so great how come the Giants and Dodgers take off?"

"I tell you smartboy, I tell you. Because there were too many black faces in the stands. That's why. For a smartboy you right dumb, Henry. Tell me somethin else. That pen pal of yours, that Lance Olsen. He know you a colored boy?"

"Well no. I don't know. It don't make no difference."

"Like hell. Hank, he in another *world*. He don't care about you. The Dodgers an Giants they say bye bye. They don't care. But *I* care. I'm lookin out for you. An I'm tellin you right here you got everything. Here. *You* can be boss."

"Shoot, we ain't even on the mainland."

"Oh Henry, Henry, this *is* the mainland. Wake up, Henry. You get with this town and you be top man. My father couldn't drive no bus. Now I'm on Fifth *Avenue*. Ezz understands. He knows what's what. Ezz, quick, give him the West Side IRT, fastes route."

Sitting at attention, rolling his head once, then pushing it back, Ezz chanted, "Terminal, South Ferry, Rector, Cortlandt, Chambers, change, Fourteenth, Twenty-third, Thirty-fourth, Times Square, Seventy-second, Ninety-six, change, One-oh-three, One-ten, One-sixteen, One-twenty-five, One-thirty-eight, One-forty-five, One-fifty-five, One-sixty-eight, One-eighty-one, Two-ten, Dyckman, Two-fifteen, Two-twenty-five, Two-forty-two, Terminal." He took a breath, opened his eyes wide, and leaned back.

"See?" beamed the Gunner. "Ezzard, what bus take you to Fort Tryon?"

"Fifth Avenue number four."

"Which one the UN?"

"Broadway number one-oh-four."

"See that Henry? See? You can do that. Bettern that. What he doin with transportation you can do with chemistry and lectricity."

"Shoot."

The Gunner smiled for the first time, stood and stretched, and took off his glasses.

"Well, that's enough for tonight," he said. "You a good boy, Hank, you be all right. Only les pull together like a real family. Okay Hank?"

"Sure."

With the same little smile, Mr. Strothers rubbed his head and walked out, shutting the door softly behind him. Henry stared at his atlas and fingered the dot at the tip of Lake Superior. Then he fingered the dots of the Giants and Dodgers. Earthquakes, the Golden Gate, terrific smog, City of the Angels. Dumb Gunner. Then his mother's voice was flowing through the door.

"Well you didn't have to be *that* hard."

And his father's, rising above hers, "Hell it's for *his* good, Ella . . ."

Next to him, rocking back and forth like he was saying his prayers, Ezz mumbling "F train, Terminal, Chambers, Hudson, Canal, Spring, West Fourth, Fourteenth . . ."

Sunday morning his father took him (just him) on six runs, up and back, Fort Tryon down to Penn Station. He sat right behind the driver's seat and listened while Mr. Strothers leaned back and in a loud, confidential voice announced and reannounced the important sights: Mt. Sinai Hospital (chemistry), Rockefeller Center (lectricity), Empire State Building (chemistry *and* lectricity). Pretty good, but nothin natural, not compared to Pike's Peak, the Great Divide or Mesabi. Still, he came on with lots of uh huhs and ain't that somethin, for always there would be a balancin time, like that quid pro quo in the French and Indian treaty. Yes sir, that a fact? . . .

That night, when released, his father patting his head and smiling, he dived into *The Great North Country* and for the thirtieth time took the run that *really* counted, from Duluth to Sault Ste. Marie. The next day at school, while the class groaned over the composition on Princeton, he whipped through the history of Minnesota.

After supper that night, while Ezz and he were washing dishes, the bell rang. Standing there in the doorway, blinking and bobbing his head was ol Mr. Wunderson. He wore his shiny black suit and his embarrassed look, like he was talking to Miss Trout.

"How do you do," Mr. Wunderson said, "I'm Henry's guidance counselor. I wonder if I might not chat with you folks for a little?"

Henry bent double over the suds, felt Ezz's tough little elbow, heard his mother murmur something nice, heard Wonder man say why thank you. Then Wonder was inside, shaking hands with the Gun, sitting beside the TV. The cruddy elbow dug into his ribs; he flicked out a fist and Ezz gasped for breath; Wonder man chatted on . . .

". . . well not exactly hooky, Mr. Strothers. More in the nature of an unofficial absence."

"He wasn't in school," the Gunner said, "he was on the hook, dammit."

"Well as his counselor, I don't quite look at it that way."

"Which way you look at it?"

"Well as a symptom of something that goes much deeper. Below the surface, as it were."

"I go below his goddam surface . . ."

His mother's rocker was creaking louder, a cheerful lisp pricked his ear with "you in trouble man," and only ALCOA held steady.

"Now, Mr. Strothers," Wonder man was saying, like in the ethics unit, "you have to realize you have an unusual boy there. With a little more . . . understanding of his ahhh unique qualities you could view this incident in its proper context. You see in Operation Buena Vista—"

"What?"

"Operation Buena Vista. A Spanish term and most

appropriate, incidentally, meaning beautiful view. We have many Puerto Rican youngsters, you know. Well, in Buena Vista, we attempt to lift our youngsters' perceptions over the horizon, so to speak. To provide meaningful experiences *outside* their life framework—"

"Mr. Wunderson, lemme explain somethin . . ."

"You see, this way we can lift them out of their environment. Now your son literally *thrills* to these experiences. So naturally when you denied him permission, he responded in his own terms. Miss Trout, his homeroom teacher, correctly perceived this and immediately brought me into the picture."

Wonder wasn't smiling, but his hands were working hard. Gunner leaned in as if he were making change.

"Mr. Wunderson," he said, "where you live?"

"Why, in Forest Hills."

"Uh huh. You come in the mornin and you go back out the Island every day after school?"

"Well not *right* after. You see some of our best guidance takes place—"

"Yeah. Well Mr. Wunderson, that's nice. Very nice. Forest Hills is real nice. But we live here. All the time. See? You go out over that bridge ever day an Henry, he still here, on this little ol rock. But *here* where he gonna make it. This *his* Bona Vista."

Wonder man began to flap his mouth like in a juvenile decency lecture. Finally he put his ideas together.

"Mr. Strothers," he said, "I have empathy for that viewpoint. Actually my living elsewhere gives me a certain valuable objectivity which, if I may say so, someone like yourself lacks. Now, Mr. Strothers, one reason I'm here is to emphasize the need for involving the school *and* the home in a cooperative effort. Frankly, I don't think this is your ahhh perception. And so we're faced with Henry's symptomatology. Now we have to work this through if we're to continue with the summer phase of Buena Vista. As you may know our youngsters correspond—"

"You mean his pen pal. That Lance Olsen?"

"Ahhh yes. Pen pal meaning link with a higher horizon. We attempt to structure a relationship whereby our youngsters can ahhh extricate themselves from their environmental fields and spend a summer in a fresh context. Now in Minnesota . . ."

"Henry in Minnesota?"

"Yes, you see, we've explored the situation with Mr. and Mrs. Olsen and—"

"You write an tell them all about Henry?"

"Well, the essentials, yes. His intellectual curiosity and his growth potential. Actually the boys themselves have made the arrangements. They seem unusually *simpatico*. And with your cooperation—"

"Mr. Wunderson, les talk to Henry. After all *he* involved here. *Hank.*"

Uh oh, Ezz diggin hard again . . . He walked slowly into the living room and gave Wonder the big handshake they had learned in group guidance. Wonder, in return, gave him the hand on the shoulder; Gunner's mouth bent down.

"Henry," Mr. Strothers said, "tell Mr. Wunderson bout your nice ride yesterday."

"We saw a lotta stuff," he said, "Empire State Building, Rockefeller Center, all kindsa stuff."

"Was it intrestin, Henry?"

"Yeah."

"Henry," Wonder man said, hand light as air on the shoulder, "how do you feel about Lance and a summer in Duluth?"

What a stupid question.

"Well," he said slowly, "we gonna hit Mesabi and goin over Wisconsin and up the Big Horn. We got a schedule."

"You see, Mr. Strothers? Do you see his involvement in terms of a fresh point of view?"

His mother's rocker had stopped and Ezz was ready to explode all over the kitchen. He felt a hand on his other shoulder, hard, tough; he played it off against the sponge.

"Why sure," Mr. Strothers said without a crack in his voice, "I want what's best for my boy, that's all. He know that. I'm all for both my boys. A hundred percent. I tell you, les jus wait an see how it go. There's time, Mr. Wunderson. Les see."

The rough hand was suddenly warm and solid, not like the damn sponge cake. Henry looked up. His father's face had cooperation, understanding and emphasy stamped all over it.

Two weeks bused by. When the class went to Philadelphia to check out the Constitution, Mr. Strothers obtained legal permission to take him on a local field trip. A whispered deal got him on the Broadway 104 and he rode from 129th to the UN with Dick Ringel giving him the tour lecture. At supper he recited the itinerary while his father beamed. Then (with a "sir") he excused himself and rescued Ezz from the torture of a simple interest problem.

While Ezz chanted *I* equal principal time rate time time, he sat down at his kneehole and got organized. Propped against the lamp was a neat blue envelope, blue as the greatest lake on the continent. He picked it up and fingered the midwestern handwriting that practically oozed iron ore. Carefully he sliced it open.

May 20

Dear Henry,

Received your letter of May 15. Thank you very much. I am fine. Everything is about the same. Well Henry about the summer Dad is going to take us to California so I'm afraid I won't be here. I guess that changes things, but we can't help it since we'll be in California. So if you don't hear from me for a while its because we'll be getting ready.

Sincerely yours,
Lance Olsen

He read it ten times. Simple interest buzzed around him. California stunk, really stunk. Then the hard, bony hand was rubbing his head.

"He give you the business?"

He looked up into understanding and cooperation.

"Oh he got a change in plans. That's all. I jus write him and we work somethin out."

The letter was in the tough hand, crumpling.

"They all the same," his father said. "All the same."

"Whachou mean, all the same?"

Mr. Strothers pulled up a chair and hunched close.

"Henry, for heavensake, snap out of it, will you? He don't want no *part* of you. That blond boy don't want no Henry Armstrong Strothers."

"Well that's somethin between Lance and me. It's probly a mistake. Don't worry, we work somethin out." Damn that Ezz, can't he *ever* learn *I* equal *prt.* Shit how stupid can you be . . .

"There ain't no *mistake.* Ezz, tell him."

"What Ezz got to do with Lance?"

Ezz looked up at Mr. Strothers who nodded and Ezz smiled, the same goddam smile when he fart in bed and try to hide it.

"You mean Ezz write to Lance? That dirty little bastid."
The whine started; his father stood up.

"Hold it boy. He do it for you."

"How you figure that?"

"Well I ask . . ."

"*You.* Goddammit, Lance is *my* friend."

"Shoot, he's no friend. He don't want no part of you now he know what you are."

"Hell he don't. Lance don't give a shit."

"Now jus calm down, Henry. Jus hold it. I know this kinda rough. I know that. But you got to learn it sometime, like I been tellin you. Now jus listen what I went an done for you. You know my cousin Roger in Canarsie. That's way out over in Brooklyn. I arrange it so you can spend the summer there. See. That ain't no city at all; it's wide open. And Roger he's a lectrician, he teach you a lot. Course you ain't gonna be no lectrician; you gonna be a engineer. But this give you some practical experience an you be one up on all the engineers. Come on now, Hank boy, pull with me, I pull with you."

He stared at his father and Ezz and then out the window. The bright red glow flung its answer over the Hudson. He shook his head with contempt.

"Donchou know nothin?" he said. "Brooklyn ain't even on the *mainland.* It's on goddam Long Island."

He lay awake very late, looking out at ALCOA. Then down at SPRY. Ezz whistlin in his doublecrossin dreams across the room. Tricks, tricks, wheelin and dealin all around him, like poor ol Hamilton. He rubbed his face where his father had cracked it. Damn. Lance's father was no goddam face cracker. The rough old rasp rose out of the bed through the wall, below it his mother's soft breathing. Shit. Even she play along. Connivers. Worse than Franny Sigel. Only the red glow and Lance were firm and now Lance was all tricked up, twisted around. Damn, he wanted to yell right out. He didn't. Instead, he just got all choky. Jesus, Lance *got* to get the story. Be squared away. He looked out at Aluminum Company of AMERICA and the choke broke up. Hell yes. Whipping the covers aside, he swung out of bed. Very careful now, though the doublecrosser never wake even if the bomb drop. He dressed and took some change out of his book bank. He stuffed the balled-up letter in his pocket and tiptoed out past all the trickers . . .

He walked over to the Drive and got the Number 5 bus right away. He dropped in small change and felt good as the driver frowned. Tough. Then he settled back and rode for half an hour, weaving in and out, up the river, over to Broadway, along Fort Washington. At 170th he crouched for action and at 178th pulled the cord. He got out and walked a block and stopped. Above him hung the great towers and swooping out and up were the cables that spun the link across the river. It was all dark, except for the tower and the bridge lights, but sighting straight across he could see the solid mass of the mainland. And next to it, the wild loopdeloop tracing of Palisades Park.

He ran over to the pedestrian walk, took a deep breath and started across. Over the narrow pathway he ran full speed, until his legs began to tie up and his side hurt. Then he stopped, gasping for breath, and glanced down. A thousand miles below, the water glinted. He jerked his head up and looked back at the city, hot, bright and beautiful. Another step and he stopped. He looked ahead for the mainland; but all he could see was thick, solid black beyond the tollbooths, hard tough black stretching all the way to Minnesota.

His knees buckled. He dropped down and crawled to the inside rail. Beside it was another hole and beneath him, nothing, just the glint. The towers began to sway and the walk swung as the cars thundered past.

He clamped onto the guard rail and saw the warm bed in his room flash against his tightly squeezed eyelids, heard the snoring through the wall. Hard and solid and a hundred percent. He thought of dumb little Ezz who needed his help. Then he saw the class: Isolina and Joseph and Katherine and Leandre, very bright and clear against the miles of black. Asking him questions, getting answers. Wunder man, Trout smiling when his hand shot up. Did The Gunner know something after all? Was Lance a goddam fuckin Aaron Burr? Was he chargin around, pullin all kindsa shit away out there in the darkness?

He felt rotten, all tied up, like the steers on the Chisolm trail were heading his way and he couldn't do a thing about it. He began to cry. He wrapped tighter around the rail as the world took off and spun around him. Up and down above the river he swung, like a cat frozen to a high, skinny pole, hung up between Duluth and 95th Street.

THE DALAI
LAMA OF
HARLEM

Daddy Thomas Heavenly looked at the baseball in his hand and the slivers of the shattered casement window that lay on his white silk suit, and he laughed, powerfully and confidently, with a knowledge of what would follow. A hushed moment descended, as of a gathering of forces, and then through the broken window darted his full expectation, in the person of a mud-caked little boy, whose body seemed a tight pack of crisscrossing wires. As Daddy stood quietly, the boy pounced on him and, with eyes focused relentlessly, grabbed the ball, ran back through a shower of broken glass, climbed down the trellis, and threw the ball with such wild violence that Daddy's arm jerked back in pain.

Ah, but he had seen the eyes, felt the animal drive, and he knew his premonition had been correct. Only twice before had he known that combination—once in Joe Louis, once in Haile Selassie. And now the same force was in action. As he watched with a smile of contentment, the riot started, rolling in a solid arm-and-leg spoke ball around the garden, with wild-eye's voice rising above all the others, "He was out, he was out, the goddam mother was out," and disengaging himself, laying about with the catlike strength of the young, unconquerable Joe. For a quiet minute Daddy enjoyed the scene; then he reached over and buzzed three times.

"Yes, Daddy," said the young man in the white gabardine suit who stood very solemn, very contained, beside the desk.

"I want that little fellow, Brother Harmony," Daddy said, pointing. "I want him now. Don't brush him off or clean him up. I want him as is."

"Yes, Daddy."

Daddy looked up at the tall thin man with the worried

face, then said, "What would you think if I told the Assembly tonight that I had found the key to my search?"

"I would think it is a cause for thanks. I would also think that we all knew some day it would happen."

"That's a wise reaction. I'm pleased." The boy lowered his eyes.

"I have plans for you, Brother, near the top. We need a tightening of the whole structure." Daddy lifted his arm. "Now, yes we do. You know it, too; you're intelligent. Well, we're making a start in that direction this minute. Fetch him."

"Yes, Daddy, thank you." With a small nod, Harmony turned and walked out.

For a short but vital period of clearance, Daddy leaned back and looked around him, at the forty-by-thirty room, the twenty-six-inch television sets, the genuine wood-burning fireplace, and the ivory chessmen always in readiness on the board. Hyde Park, he had once remarked at Open House, had nothing like this, and Mrs. Roosevelt had gazed about her and replied, "Mr. Heavenly, it doesn't even come *close.*" Sitting behind his desk in this critical moment, he thought back to Mrs. Roosevelt and the President and the good fight they had made together back in the glory days when they had battled the wicked, each in his own way. He thought on how much he owed Mrs. Roosevelt for what was about to occur; it was because of her (or his professional admiration for the way she handled her operation) that in five minutes he would be face to face with his logical worldly heir. For Daddy had instantly grasped the possibilities that hung brightly in her yearly custom of inviting the tough boys of Children's Village to Hyde Park, and following her magnanimous example, he had rounded up the far tougher boys of 120th Street, from Broadway to Second Avenue, to be *his* guests at Starry Acres. At seventy-three Daddy Heavenly had begun to think about succession (even as David and Caesar) and the glorious notion had taken hold that somewhere among those hellcats trampling his rhododendron once a year would appear the most exciting choice in the world (far surpassing the cruel lottery of the temptings of the flesh), just as he had materialized out of an acre of Louisiana mud, a natural boy, unschooled, unharnessed, but bursting with the power. And now, after eight years of patience, the omen he desired had crashed through the window—and Daddy Heavenly surely knew it. . . . Cleared and calmed, he focused on the paneled door, and when he was ready (not a moment before), it slid back and the pack of wires with eyes walked through. On his face was the mud of Daddy's garden; on his sweatshirt clung a crushed white aster. He was crumpled and sweat-streaked. But the face. Ah, the face was alive and thoughts roved behind those great, probing eyes. What a promising mess of dross, Daddy thought, as the boy stood in the center of all that beauty and looked steadily at him.

"Come here, boy," he said. With his eyes fixed calmly (a good sign), the boy moved in a step. "What is your name, boy?"

"Samson DeBaron." The voice was high and thin, but very clear.

"Excellent name. Fine evocations there. How are you, Sam?"

"Samson."

"Ah yes, of course. Samson. Tell me, Samson, who are you named for?"

"Why you wanna know, coach?"

"You just tell me, son," Daddy said, his eyes strong on the boy, "and don't ask why."

The interlocking wires stiffened; a look of careful friendliness (interpreted instantly) covered his face.

"My mother read it in a book."

"Fine answer. And a very good book it was. Does your mother read a lot, Samson?"

"You soundin on my mother?"

"Why no, of course not. Obviously your mother is a fine woman. Relax, Samson, I'm not a Philistine about to eat you. Or cut off your hair." He smiled. "Although you could stand a trim." The boy remained stiffly at attention; plenty of hard-core spirit there. "Do you know who I am, Samson?" Daddy said in his kindliest voice.

"You with the P.A.L.?"

"No, although that's a very worthwhile organization. Think on it. The name of this place, Starry Acres. The little gold angel on the lawn holding a sign that says 'The Retreat of Heaven.' You listen to the radio. Who am I, Samson?"

"I don know, coach."

"I'm Daddy Heavenly."

"Thas nice, coach."

"And that is how you must address me in future. With both names. Later on, when you have made progress, you can call me Daddy."

"Uh huh. Whachou want with me, coach?"

"Daddy Heavenly."

"Yeah yeah, Daddy Heavenly, whachou want, Daddy Heavenly?"

Rising slowly, Daddy stood for a moment and then walked to the boy and rested his hand lightly but firmly, so the tingle would pass through to the thin shoulder. "How would you like to remain here, Samson?"

"Whafor?"

"A good question. Look about you, Samson. In your wildest imaginings did you ever think that something like this could one day be yours? That is, transmitted into your keeping? Think. Truth, my boy, *is* stranger than fiction. Our truth. Samson, you could stay here and wear fine clothes and be someone important. Make your presence count. Just as I. You could *run* this place and others like it. Not right away, of course, but one day. Think of it, Samson."

"I got a home."

"Of course. And it will be well provided for, I assure you. But Samson, this has a meaning that transcends. Look at me, son. That's it, straight up. It's a little early, but do you feel something? Anything? Just relax and receive." He pressed his hand down. "What do you feel, boy?"

"Nothin."

Daddy merely smiled. "That's all right," he said, patting the erect head. "I don't want to push. It will come in its own good time. We'll move slowly, carefully. I want you here, Samson. You'll understand in due time." His voice grew brisk. "Now I'll make all necessary arrangements. Just depend on Daddy." He buzzed and Harmony materialized at the door. The boy looked up at Daddy, then across to the tall man blocking the door, and back again.

"Sure, coach," he said calmly, "anythin you says . . ."

Daddy told the Assembly that night and they had an all-time ball of rejoicement. Samson was presented, scrubbed up shiny, in a brown ivy-league suit, with white shirt and pencil-slim tie. Over his breast pocket, on his shirt, his tie, and on his B.V.D. shorts were embroidered two embracing gold angels. He clutched his hands over his head like Sugar Ray; the Assembly roared its approval; and he was hustled off for a refreshing night's sleep in preparation for the first day, while the festivities reigned till Dawn Number One of Daddy Heavenly's New Era.

The first morning his training began in the Chapel of Repose, under the close supervision of Brothers Harmony and Progress, while Daddy got on the phone and tended to legal and personal details. The original Mr. DeBaron, as far as his skip-tracers could find, had long since melted into the streets, but at noon Mrs. Leona DeBaron was identified in George's Hideaway Lounge on Eighth Avenue and 129th Street and whisked up to Starry Acres, where Daddy stated his case briefly, smoothly, and with no nonsense. Mrs. DeBaron whimpered a bit, held out for sixty a week, settled for fifty, cried bitterly over her squirming son, and weaved her way elegantly to the waiting Cadillac. Then Daddy dismissed his legal and financial advisers and personally conducted the boy on a lecture tour of the printing plant, where *I Believe in Me* was turned out—five thousand copies a month, in five languages—and *Heavenly Chatter* was composed each week. He followed with a turn around the property, from Peace Lake to the terraced gardens, beginning at the bottom with Hope and ascending up to Light. They came back along the Great White Way, on each side of which perched the little Dove Houses where the Sisters and Brothers lived, with no silly nonsense, *ever*. And finally a walk through the Fields of Plenty and the Good Barns, where the Friendly Beasts dwelled, surrounded by their up-to-date machinery. "We are all," Daddy said with a note of pride, "perfectly self-sufficient here, outside and inside. We are beholden to no one, to nothing, except of course the message. Well, Samson, what do you think now?"

"It's awful damn quiet."

"Watch your language, son. That's correct. It is quiet.

You will find that after a time the quiet goes to the heart of your being. It will cleanse and purify you. Then you will be ready. But you must work very hard. Harder than you have worked in your entire life. You must study *I Believe in Me* over and over until it sinks into your bones and nerves. Then you will see I didn't receive all of this free of charge." He stroked the neatly clipped head. "Here we are, boy. Now you go over to Brother Harmony and do exactly as he says. Lean on him; he's a fine man." He gave Samson a gentle push.

"All right, Brother," he said crisply, "he's all yours. Get him into some decent work clothes. That simple cotton robe I designed. Stencil "The Boy" over the angels. Start him out on history. He's coming along, but he needs understanding. His eyes are still asking some big questions." Turning, he walked quickly back to the Retreat, feeling younger and stronger than he had in years.

Dimming the lights for his afternoon meditation break, he leaned back in the lounger, turned on the vibration juice, and felt the rhythm buzz up a collection of highly satisfying responses. This he needed. Daddy craved emotional exercise like children needed play. It stretched him up, tightened his thinking, developed his sense of inner communion. He hadn't even realized how blurry his wellsprings had become till he had swung into this project. Once again he was building, creating instead of consolidating, like the old victory days of the Crusades through 125th Street, up St. Nick's to the Polo Grounds and over the viaduct to the Bronx. And out to Coney Island and Union City. Lightning in a bottle. But this was better. This was Daddy and *Daddy* himself for all time, spreading the message with new, trained stock, with bigger and finer presses, and one day the finest dream of all, the Heavenly TV Net-

work. Oh yes. Samson was the one. Underneath those layers of street dirt and dark cellars the boy had oneness, the
Central Strength. Oh indeed yes. A strength forged on the
hot white streak of 125th Street, in the rock-and-rolling
Apollo . . . Daddy threw the Barca into high and rode it like
Tom Mix breaking in Tony. Then when he had it mastered
he snapped it off and externalized; the rhythm of success
—hot then cool. He got up and walked to the color console
and turned to the twi-night doubleheader and sat back for
the other end of his balance control. He lit his pipe and the
old familiar stadium flashed on. And packing it, that yap-
ping, squirming mob. He blew three perfect halos. What a
deep pleasure not to fight through all the push and smell;
he inhaled the freshness of the room, tinged delicately with
the embers in the fireplace . . . Mantle hit one and the roar
filled the room. Deep and solid. The kind of roar he used
to pull, young powerful Tommy Wilson, fresh out of the
dunghills. Sixty thousand throats. Why, he was a bigger
draw than Mantle. Me oh my, just thirty-five miles down
there hung all that wildness, and around it, rising on all
sides, the iron and hot cement pressing the ferment together like a Fleischmann's yeast cake. All that throbbing
and spilling over that he could flick off with his gold-encir-
cled pinky. Why, he could smell it through the screen. He
smiled and got up. With his pinky he delicately turned the
dial, then sat down. A smooth face filled the screen. A
deadly serious face under carefully shaped hair, featuring
a precise moustache. That same oilsmooth face gleaming at
him everywhere he turned. That same name, prefabricated
and ridiculous. Martin Luther and King. Oh Mama Heavenly, what an insult to intelligence! He was sitting there,
Mr. Luther King, calm as a British diplomat, probably in
a bus seat he carried around with him, talking neatly and

softly, like a high school teacher. But don't let that easy voice fool you, no indeed. This one could instigate, incite, uproot . . . Oh yes he could. Sit-ins and sit-ups and every other damn kind of sitting. Hell, *we* had sit-down strikes in 1933 when the oilman was drooling in his pablum. Nothing remarkable about sitting, just fold the body at the pressure points. But this one, he had them stirred up and shaking about rights and wrongs and a million other downhill things that spelled hate. Hell, they should be drinking in peace and light, those tight, hot faces, not the venom of a false prophet. . . . He stared hard into that delicately soft moonface, puzzling over its centrality . . .

A door opened and he felt a tall, thin presence. And in good time: the moustache on a balloon was reaching his internals. He closed his eyes and threw his mind as a ventriloquist does his voice. Check. The old assessment faculty had stood up again. Harmony. Harmony beside him, quiet and dignified, *really* dignified. Except his hands. His hands were drywashing each other and that wasn't standard; Harmony was usually all harmony.

"Well, Brother, what is it?"

"Please pardon my interrupting."

"All right, son, what is it?"

"It's the boy."

"Yes, Brother?"

"He's gone."

"What the hell are you talking about?"

"Oh Daddy, the boy is gone. I turned my back to clip a dead rose and when I turned around he was gone."

For a long, quiet moment Daddy sat there. Just sat. Then he moved, with all the thrust and force that young chained Bull Wilson ever had. Mr. Luther King's low, honeyed voice was still mocking him as that powerful leg kicked in the screen.

For a whole night and day, Daddy lay inert. The terrific Heavenly Drive, the great thrust, seemed to have shriveled up. The Brothers and Sisters, tiptoeing around the mansion, looking anxiously toward the closed windows, marveled at the extent to which a great heart could crack. He did not eat or drink. He lay on his huge chaise longue, staring at the crystal chandelier. Until evening and then night closed around the Acres and all the spotlights were dimmed and the music cut off at Harmony's orders. Then, and only then, in the new gathering blackness, did the first stirrings seep into the great head, for night and blackness were Daddy's old familiar garments. The head moved ever so slightly and with it the Awareness began to shape itself, deep within the pain. It sharpened and hardened and plunged out through the window and into the woods and along the roads until it could pick out Samson like a pair of Caddy headlights. Finally, a thin smile broke the band around Daddy's face. . . . The little devil would beat out any pair of headlights this side of paradise. Hell, *we* can *smell* the sheriff and his stupid signals a half mile away, can't we, boy, and go shooting off into the trees and lay there with our belly in our mouth till the stupid lights and the drooling dogs go crashing by. . . . Samson would know. He would be swearing about now, that magnificent foulmouth, and tearing off the goddam boss clothes. The goddam motherin dress, that's what that boy would say. That's right. . . . Daddy's Faculty arched further out like a tracer bullet, over the trees and through the air, and dropped down and loped alongside the wildcat in the mother silk drawers and fancy paper shoes, no goddam good for running. Lord, he was tough, that boy! And foul. And *certain*. That's the *only* way, ain't it, boy? We can do anything with those weapons, can't we, boy? Any motherin thing . . . Oh yes, that one would go forever, or till he dropped. Daddy groaned and sat up and planted his feet on the carpet. He rose and stood there, sweating and exhausted from the chase as Samson plunged toward the dying sun. He began to walk around the room. He grabbed a towel and unbuttoned his shirt and dried himself. Okay, boy, okay, keep going; that's the way we have got to do it. Just the two of us; only we know how it is. I'm with you all the way, boy; just remember, I've been there, too. I've got all your cards and an ace of my own. Oh you're making it worth my while, sonny, yes indeed . . . He snapped on all the lights and shoved the Awareness back into his head. Then he doled out his special protective force, his guideline to safety, no matter where Samson was . . . "Just remember, boy," he said out loud, buttoning his shirt, "I ain't no sheriff."

Restored and better than ever, Daddy was all action and reaction. Big picture, little picture. Pacing up and down, back and forth, checking and rechecking, flipping switches, coordinating the whole complex operation like General Ike on D day. Then, at ten in the morning, the insistent buzz came from the Outer Sanctum. Swooping toward a relief map, he paused in flight and switched on the intercom, pulling in Sister Grace Note's agitated voice.

"Oh Daddy, Daddy," Sister whined, "some high official is on the phone."

"Dammit, what the hell does he want?"

"I don't know, Daddy, he won't tell me."

"Who the hell is he?"

"I don't know, Daddy, he won't tell me. He insists on talking to the head official."

"Can't you tell him I'm busy, Sister?"

"Oh Daddy, I told him." (Damn. Good-hearted but helpless.) "What should I do, Daddy?"

"Okay dammit, don't cry, Sister, plug him in." He turned on the big telephone voice unit. "Shoot," he barked, "I'm listening."

"Mr. Heavenly?" the voice filled the room, high and anxious.

"Yes, yes."

"This is Vice-Warden McCarthy of Sing Sing Prison."

"Yes, Warden."

"Vice-Warden."

"Sorry. Vice-Warden. Say, I'm tied down today with some pressing business. Could I send my group over?"

"Mr. Heavenly, I think we have one of your people here."

"What did you say?"

"One of your people. A youngster, about ten years of age. He's wearing a nightgown with 'Starry Acres' stenciled on the back. . . . Hello, Mr. Heavenly . . ."

"Yes, I'm listening." Daddy sat down. "Where did you find him?" His voice was soft and controlled.

"Well, he broke into our institution."

"He *what*?"

"Well, we found him asleep in the corner of a recreation area."

"He broke into *Sing Sing*?"

"I guess you could say that."

Daddy got up and walked around the room with the portable mike in his hand. With his toe he took a swipe at some broken glass that hadn't been swept up. "Holy Jesus," he breathed.

"Whatwasat, Mr. Heavenly? Say, what do you want done at this end? We'd like to cooperate with you people."

"Oh, yes, yes, thank you, Warden. Vice-Warden."

"You want us to drive him out to your . . . estate?"

"No, thank you, no. Wait a minute. We'll come and fetch him. How is he? I mean, is he damaged or anything?"

"No sir, he's in A-one condition. I had my medic check him over. Just a few third-degree scratches. We fed him and he asked to watch the softball game and we complied. We like to display the type of thing that's going on up here. He's even playing in the game."

Carefully holding the switch down, Daddy said, "Jesus-ChristAlmighty," and flipped it back up. "All right, Vice-Warden, very good. Just keep him occupied. We'll be right over. And I certainly do appreciate this."

"That's perfectly all right. We like to cooperate; it's good for our people. Drop in yourself. Nice talking to you, Mr. Heavenly. Over and out."

Hot damn, Sing Sing, Daddy thought, smiling into the phone. He hit those walls and he took them, that hot little monkey. He's unstoppable. Man, he can do it all, give it back in spades and ram it down their throats. Why, he might even make them forget Daddy . . .

In fifteen minutes three white Cadillacs had swept down on the city of Ossining and up to the prison gates. In fifteen more minutes the Cadillacs were purring contentedly outside the Retreat. And in five minutes more exactly, Brother Harmony was standing stiffly before the great desk.

"He's outside," Brother said quietly, and Daddy swiveled around from the lake view and a brief period of analysis.

"How is he?" he said. "I mean *really?*"

"He resisted me violently," Brother said.

"The little wildcat. What else?"

"He said he wanted to stay there."

"In Sing Sing?"

"Yes. I asked him that. He replied—and these are his exact words—'I goes good here.' " Brother Harmony was sweating a little and his jacket pocket was torn; a thin scratch, straight as a furrow, ran from his eyebrow to his mouth. The wild little pig . . . "All right, you did very well. Thank you. Now send him in. And take the afternoon off." Harmony turned quickly and walked out; a flurry of whispers, which Daddy carefully ignored, hissed through the door. Then Samson walked in slowly, dressed in shorts and socks. He was all hard, crisscrossing gutstring, from neck to belly; his arms and legs were covered with mercurochrome. His face was a careful zero. Not his eyes. "Sit down, son," Daddy said.

"I wanna stand."

"All right, son, you can stand. Well, so you ran away. You know, I can understand that. I ran away myself. Six times by the time I was your age. I recall each flight."

"Yeah."

"The only difference was I ran away to build something. Now, son, you don't have to run. See? You have it all built up, right here. All right, so you went and did it and got it out of your system. Now suppose we settle down to some serious work. I'm going to forgive and forget, Samson." He stood, walked over and dropped his hand on the sloping shoulder. Oh my, he was thin. He held out his other hand.

"When I'm goin home, Mr. Heavenly?" Samson said, ignoring the hand.

Daddy sighed. "Samson, Samson, this *is* your home. Some day this will all be *yours.*" Daddy paced to the end of the room and back. "You're starting to vex me a little, boy. Sit down."

"I likes to stand."

"Sit down."

His eyes full on Daddy, Samson sat gingerly on the edge of the lounger, his feet dangling off the floor. Swiftly Daddy cranked the chair so the feet came down flush; then he sat on the corner of his desk. He waited until he felt the moment. "Samson boy," he said, relaxing into his confidential voice, "let me tell you a little anecdote. That's a story with a point." His voice was mellow and round, the voice that had scored so deeply at the White House. A council-of-the-world voice all for this little boy. "Samson," he said, "let me tell you about a place called Tibet. That's far off over in Asia, near a place called China. Now in this Tibet, they have a very big man running things; you could say he was a God man. That he comes straight from Heaven. That's right. He is *heavenly.* They call this person the Dalai Lama. Doll-lye La-mah. Now this important personage is smart. Very smart. He knows a lot of things regular people don't know. He knows for instance he won't live forever. And he knows something else. He knows," Daddy's voice moved down and in, "that somewhere there's another Dalai Lama waiting to step into his shoes. Only this second fellow doesn't know it yet, see. Now, why doesn't he? Because he's very small, just a little baby maybe, or a little kid running around the mountains of Tibet. So the big Dalai goes out and looks everywhere and then one day he finds the little guy and he can be poor as a churchmouse, down and out, but he picks him up. Understand? And from that day on, they all groom this poor kid to be the big man. The *Dalai Lama.* Now Samson, hear this. It is very important." His eyes dug in. "That is the best way to do these things. I've given it a great deal of thought and I know. You are a smart boy, Samson; you see my meaning?" Daddy slipped off the desk and stood over the lounger; he looked down from his full six foot three. "You see who *you* can be?"

Samson gazed hard into the force bending over him. "I ain't no chink," he muttered. Daddy shook his head. "Oh my my, that is not very brotherly." He looked into the upturned face. "Oh but you've got a lot to learn. And unlearn. We've got to clean all that poison out of your system before you're ready."

Suddenly he reached down beneath the skinny arms and hauled the paper-light body up so their eyes were level. "But son, I'm telling you straight and true," he said. "You have *got* it. You. Now you put your faith and trust in me and I'll put you over. I will make you the biggest Lama in this entire *country.*"

Samson hung in midair, perfectly still, like a puppy stretched out and helpless. Then he put his hands on his hips. His body stiffened and the breath rose in him and blew up his belly, his chest, and his neck, till the seams stood out hard and black.

"*You sonuvabitch,*" he screamed, "*I don't wanna be no god.*"

Daddy was writing his column when Harmony walked in the next morning, but he dropped his pen instantly and stood up. "Do come in, Brother," he said warmly. "I'm so glad you stopped by. I've been meaning to ask you in. And here you are." He smiled and walked around the desk. "How are you?"

"Fine, thank you."

Daddy pulled up a chair. "Sit down, son."

"I think I will stand, thank you."

Must be a ban on sitting all of a sudden, Daddy thought jovially; better not tell Mr. Luther and King. He looked softly at Harmony for an indicator. With Harmony lately it was the hands. But they were at peace, comfortable as two sleeping birds. Daddy sat down in front of his desk. "Well, son, how's it going?"

"I have a report I want to make," Harmony said, his voice velvet soft.

"Good. I always enjoy your reports."

"I want to report," Harmony said, his hands awakening, "that the Apprentice in Training has run away again."

Daddy uncoiled from the chair. "Give it to me again," he snapped, feeling his pocket of warmth burst.

"The Apprentice in Training. He has run . . ."

"Yeah yeah, what the hell, is this a goddam game? You telling me that every day? Whothehell does that little stinkweed think he is?"

"I just wanted to report . . ."

"All right dammit I heard you. Do I have to supervise every damn thing around here? All right all right, let's not stand around sucking our fingers. Ring the goddam bell."

"It happened last night."

The hard rock in Daddy's belly moved up and out and exploded in his hand. His fist slugged the desk and the thick glass top cracked end to end. *"Why are you telling me now?"* he roared. "He goes last night and you tell me *now?* Goddammitohell mister I gave *you* the responsibility. I gave it to you. *Direct.*"

"It's all right," Harmony said quietly. "I found him."

Daddy leaned forward to pick up the secret; damn, this boy was talking in secrets. "You just say you found him?"

"Yes."

The chair got under Daddy just in time. "Oh Brother Harmony," he said, shaking his head, "don't be so efficient. Please. I mean, you can tell me the second thing first and I'll still respect your organizational talents." The iron-hard meat-edge of his hand throbbed as he lit up and sat back.

"Where'd you find the little weasel?"

"At the bottom of a slag pit near Briarcliff. His neck was broken."

Once before Daddy had felt it. On the Louisiana gang, when the guard billied him in the crotch and kicked his head silly when he dropped; his eardrums were smashed and he heard voices through cushions of blood, softly, thickly, and in hot waves. Now his gut and head were bursting; his ears were gummed up; he kept pulling at them to release the sound. But banging him from the inside, like the billy, was the same phrase: Don't make him repeat it, mister, you heard right. With a great accumulation of will, he tried banishing Harmony; but then he opened his eyes and Harmony was still there, very quiet, very efficient, waiting for Daddy. He pushed past the words and the pressure and said, "Where is he?"

"In the Chapel. I made all the necessary arrangements."

"Oh my my my my my. Oh my my my my . . ."

"He seemed quite happy when I found him." Harmony's voice was droning in and out at him. "He was facing the city and one leg was bent under him like a runner's. He really looked quite happy." That voice, straight and matter-of-fact—"I'll take two pounds of butter." "The bomb is dropping, mister. No, over there." It kept flowing toward him like mud. Oh, Harmony could stand beefing up in the voice department. The mud stopped; then it formed and hardened all around him. "Daddy Heavenly," the mud said, "I am leaving now. Permanently. I would like to say goodbye and thank you."

Daddy was trying; he was trying very hard, but what the hell was going on around here? Didn't he have enough burden with poor Samson laying up there with that tough, proud neck snapped? Dammitohellnow they could just stop all this damn nagging and hurting. The dead weight of his head came out of his hands. "What did you say?"

"I am leaving, Daddy."

Damn damn damn, Daddy needed his people when *he* needed them. Here and now. "What are you saying, boy? Just what are you *doing* to me? You trying to hurt Daddy? You *blaming* him? Is *that* what you're doing?"

"No, Daddy. It wasn't your fault. Not really. I . . . well, I don't think you could help it. Let us leave it at that. But I am finished." Oh that hard, final note, slicing like a bugle through Daddy; the Scottsboro boy had that note . . .

"Now, Brother, don't say that. Why are you saying that? Look, son, I am humbling myself. Daddy Heavenly. Stay with me."

"I have to go."

"Go? Where? Where you going?"

"Well, I'm starting south . . ."

"Oh that's it. That is it." Daddy's voice took off like Sister Grace Note's, but he couldn't catch it. "That Martin Luther and his college boys. He's got you crazy too. What will you do, boy, take a bus ride down to Montgomery and sit in the gutter? Is that what? That is where you will wind up, boy, in the gutter, mark these words. You want that? Oh they must have got poor Samson crazy, too . . ."

"No, no, Daddy. My goodness, control yourself. I am

merely going to New York. I don't know what I will do right away. Then, yes, I suppose I will work with one of the action groups there. Maybe, maybe even the Black Muslims. Daddy, I must get on the *inside.*"

Words, words, choking, mocking him . . . He activated his benevolence. "Look here, Harmony. See? I am very calm. See that? Now, just listen to Daddy. That man *down there* is a troublemaker. He is a phony troublemaker. They are all smartass troublemakers. Harm baby, that is *not* the way, their way. That way is all hate and bitterness. Love and peace, that is the ticket, baby, the winning ticket. Harmony, you listen, you listen to this now. Stick with Daddy and we take it nice and easy and I promise you something. A reward. You know Daddy and his promises. I promise you— on Mama Heavenly's grave—that *you* will step into Samson's shoes. That is correct. You and me. We will make it up to the little fellow. Maybe, maybe it was supposed to happen this way. Yes indeed, I know about these things. Harm, we'll overhaul the whole operation. I know you have criticisms, I've seen them in your eyes. We'll trim off the fat, get down to rock bottom. I am *promising,* Harmony . . ."

"I would like you to call me Lewis McNeil. That is my name."

"You're *Harmony.* You're my harmonious right hand. You came here troubled and *I* gave you peace."

"Yes, Daddy, and for that I thank you. Now I must go." He held up his hand as if *he* were in charge. "Daddy, let me tell you something significant. After I found Samson I put him in the car, the Cadillac, so big he was almost lost inside. Well, I drove down to Ossining. To Sing Sing. And I got out, with Samson lying there on the back seat. He looked like a little dead cat. You know how they smile sometime?

Well, I looked at the prison. It was growing dark and it was time to get back, but I kept sitting there. And you know why? Sing Sing looked so cozy."

"Harmony, you stop that. You're upset, son. This was a real shock, that's why you're talking so foolish."

Harmony sighed. He shook his head slowly and looked gently at Daddy. Then he said, oh, so softly, "Daddy, I let him go."

For a long time Daddy sat in his thick leather chair. Just before he jammed his mind shut, he flashed the picture of the boy working Harmony over (with that hard, direct strength), boring into his soft conscience with that irresistible drive. He even saw the moment of the break as poor defenseless Harmony smiled and turned away and counted all the roses, one by one. And he slammed the door hard.

Then, as quietly as Lewis McNeil ever spoke, quiet as M. Luther King at his quietest, without raising his head, he said, "All right, Lewis. It is all right." Oh, he still had his Awareness faculty. In all that numbness, it still worked. He felt the cool, withdrawn presence gaze down, felt it turn, and felt it float out of the room. Felt desertion. Felt all the space around him . . .

He was in the middle of that nothing for a long time, was Daddy Heavenly, until it was very late and the Brothers and Sisters had long since gone to sleep, and it was just him and the insects outside the window, banging and winging for the light. And the boy in the Chapel. Finally, with a mighty heave, he roused up and turned on the television for a little friendship; but the screen jabbed "While the City Sleeps" at him and he turned it off with a cry of alarm. Then he snapped off the light, so now he didn't even have those angry hot creatures for company. Only the boy. Oh Mama. He sank. Far down, deeper even than on the night before

the Crusade for the Bronx, or the terrible Fast Day to Save
the Heights. Clear down to hungry little Tommy Wilson
and his terrific aloneness in the black Louisiana night. And
while he filled up with aloneness like it was potatoes and
turnips, he felt great jagged tears around his heart, and
through them began to slip the Grandeur, the Splendor,
the Nobility, the great investment of thirty-five years. He
fought to hang on, oh he fought with all the tricks and turns
in Daddy's bag; but they moved out like a wide, slow moun-
tainslide, until he was cleaned out, empty, scooped open
for the worst thing in history. Then he began to shake and
shiver, just as poor little Tommy shook under the stars; and
he was terrified all over again. Oh please leave him alone,
Samson, he didn't want that power back; he was through,
finished with it, sweet Daddy deserved a break after all the
sweat and struggle. Let Harmony fight. And Luther the
King, he was in love with jails . . . Listen, Winnie Churchill
was living like a king in sunny France. Franklin Delano
would be relaxing in Hyde Park with his disciples. Daddy
Heavenly was on *that* level, right up there; he had given, he
had earned it, too. Look Samson, we'll make a deal; I'll
bring all the poor bastards in Sing Sing up here once a week
. . . twice a week . . . Oh he struggled mightily, as befitted
a personage of his station. For the first time in twenty years,
he got down on his knees. He fought until he could hang
on no longer and all that great muscle and nerve sagged.
And then the power charged. Straight into the vacuum like
that cop's billy. The power that once put him inside each
head in the crowd, made each heartbeat his heartbeat. With
that power, Paul Robeson said, he could have been the
greatest actor in the world. Or another Emperor Jones. Oh
it was strong. It shoved him into the clodhopping shoes of
the smashed-up boy in the Chapel, scrambling and scratch-

ing his way back to the darkness. Into the great head and the sledgehammer muscles and the huge belly, the power crammed all the peeling plaster behind every rotten brick, every melting tar roof, every cockroach crawling over every filthy baby. It filled him up with every stinking bottle of compressed life down there, fizzing, spurting, shooting over like a shook-up Coca-Cola. Rummies, droolers, screechers, bleeders, cats and cat houses all latched on. He couldn't help himself and he damn well knew it, the Prophet of Heaven, the True Light, the Him Above All. Little Tommy Wilson out there in the Chapel had won. The Heavenly Person bent forward and vomited up the sugar of all the plush, lost years. Then with the power full and clean in him, he just got up, walked out of his mansion, and started down toward all the magnificent bone-misery of the city.

THE
DOUBLE
SNAPPER

1

Six months after he came to Apex, in answer to the memo "Please. Here. Now." MacBean walked into the red-leathered office at precisely the moment that the great red leather chair swiveled away from him, pointed down Madison Avenue and floated the suggestion that he sit down and make himself nice and comfortable. Savoring the exquisite timing, MacBean sat down on a leather-covered chair with enfolding wings and waited. He counted two beats, a wisp of smoke, the creak of the great chair, waited one more beat, and watched as P. Nelsma, tucked neatly into the corner of the red, swung into view. P. Nelsma braked with a tiny foot, held, took the pipe out of his mouth and said gently, "Something really stinks, Mac." And MacBean, who had early recognized his partnership in the ritual, held another beat, just long enough for the interval to say Oh? Such as?

"I'll tell you what stinks, Mac," said P. Nelsma. "Here it is. I am here for one reason, right? Right. And that is for us to stop being number two. You know what number two is, right?" MacBean winced and nodded. "You know," said P. Nelsma. "Ergo, *you* are here for us to stop being number two."

"We used to be number three," MacBean said. "And before that, number four."

"True." P. Nelsma rotated 360 degrees and coasted throughtfully to a stop. "Still, it is not engraved in the Koran that this network shalt not be number one."

Reviewing the late-show litheness of the song-and-dance man balanced before him, MacBean concluded that he had lost none of his style.

"True," he said. "It is not."

"Mac," said the thoughtful hoofer, "I brought you in here, did I not?"

"Yep."

"And I made you number one VP. Thrust you high up there above the mob . . ."

"They're not too bright, Nels."

"All right. That's not the point. They can't help themselves. They're encrusted. The point is, I said you're my boy. I said the hell with his messy background, I want him in that office."

"Messy background, but it proves I'm literate."

"Don't be insubordinate. You wanna go back to educational TV?"

"No, please, I'll be good." MacBean's head dipped. When it rose, P. Nelsma was perched on the end of his desk, gazing down at him.

"Kenyon College," said Nelsma, "one thing they never taught you squarish types out West is a thing called intuition."

"That's an inborn trait, Nels, like a congenital heart murmur . . ."

"All right, I murmur. I shout."

"Yes, Nels?"

"My shouting intuition is telling me something. I will tell you what it tells me. It tells me that Billy the Kid and Wyatt Earp are dead."

"Oh?"

"And likewise Quantrill's Raiders and Long George Custer. At least for the time being."

"Well, I suppose there has been some overexposure."

"Dead. They are dead. And so is World War One. And Two."

"And the Civil War?"

"Dead."

"How about the Spanish-American War and the Mexican War?"

"War is hump. We've milked it dry." P. Nelsma floated to his red couch and hung on an arm. "I know what you're going to say. *Able Baker* has a ten-three, *Yankee Soldier You Die* an eleven-one. Strictly momentum. They're dead."

"And your intuitive heart shouts make a move before they're buried."

"You read me beautifully, Kenyon." P. Nelsma got up and walked to his desk and sat on it. "Very frankly, I'm tired of Worldwide dancing on my behind. The time is now. You're my creativity department. You've been gestating for six months, right?"

"Right."

"You wanted all those little magazine writers nobody reads. I got them for you, right?"

"Right."

P. Nelsma's red telephone flew up in a perfect arc and clamped onto his ear, indicating end of interview. He looked down solemnly.

"Okay, so create."

In his office MacBean picked up his Executary microphone, leaned back, closed his eyes, clicked on and monotoned: "Order of the day, opus three . . . ahhhh . . .

> *Have to break out, have to get catholic*
> *D day's passé and so is that rat dick.*

Jessie you're messy, ho Jonas Salk
our pulse you can't find, our seams you don't caulk.
So . . . shatter the mold, those items so fancy
let's see . . . For Medic *is ded* (sic!) *and glop all romancey,*
ahhh . . . Milties and Hillties, good old Bonanza
tax all our wit, strain our . . . credanza.
Yeah, the hell with tornadoes, that charged-up
        white knight,
We got to get with it, now isn't that right?

RIGHT."

He clicked off and let the laughter bubble up un-recorded, then removed the band and slid it into an envelope with opus one and two and filed under Personal. Slipping another band over the rollers, he picked up the mike, frowned into it and clicked on.

"Sally, pick this up fast and shoot it out to the writers. . . . Memo. From Grayson MacBean. Subject, new, vital material. Text. Mr. Nelsma is disturbed by lack of freshness, *jism* in major continuity series, which will result inevitably in sagging Trendex, Nielsen. I'm inclined to agree. This could be break we have waited for, chance to assert common belief that originality, talent, ideas and—underline—marketability are not necessarily incompatible. Caps last three words. New paragraph. Let's clean out cobwebs. Let ideas foam up. Tease them out. Then posthole. Underline, cap that. I know you can do it. Remember my door is always open, don't hesitate to hit me. Okay Sally."

Replacing the mike, he slapped the desk hard, wheeled around, landed on his toes and walked out to lunch.

2

By Friday the outlines began to come in. The first and longest was from Istvan Stulpski, whom he had recruited on the London scouting trip. His reaction card listed Stulpski as "Traditionalist, classical bkground; tension poised on twin prongs of hatred for Germany, Russia; could produce if and when analysis tips scales." Stulp submitted *The New Adventures of Joseph K.* . . . "Groping, fumbling, fever-ridden search in modern world contex. [Ouch!] Switch accusation to values. Suggest Joseph be Southern Californian, perhaps wetback or *bracero,* in which case José K. Poss. locales: San Diego, San Fernando Vall., Tijuana, Centr. America, Honolulu, etc. Have him eliminate local dictator each episode, e.g. goddam druggist, big farmer, feedman, etc."

MacBean sighed and penciled a neat "Thank you, very interesting. Some problems here in identification for Amer. viewers. Also possible conflict with José Jimenez. Keep punching." And on his card he typed "Still hasn't come out of it."

He turned to Gibby Bergman, the *Washington Square Review* alum, whose react card said "Remarkable drive. Frenzy? Could be, but worth a shot. One room, black coffeed, 4 A.M. ventilator, gut spiller. Play father figure for this one." Gibby had handed in *Les Fleurs du Mal,* verse drama built around inner life of Buddy Delaire, cab driver–poet–prober into "core matters of this stinking, reeking, hellish, crap-filled world . . . ain't seen you lately; you mad? I do something? What? Come around Sat, 4 chix dying meet you, very zoftik, guar. action, or if you want change your luck . . . Know perfect Buddy D: Me."

"*Gracias* man," he wrote in red. "It really grabs, but question if John Q. and Mary are tuned in. You know? Also policy here (which I support) to separate assignments. And personal aside—Stay away from acting, man. Nurse the wound, let it fester, don't externalize and dissipate all that talent which I know you possess. Give the bow something to work with. Course I'm not t.o.'d. Got problems, too, you know? Promise see you soon."

On Monday afternoon Sally dropped Marty Broad's memo into the basket. It was smeared, scratched out, curled up on itself. Like rough, tough, poor little Marty, "Young Algren, worlds of potential; needs solid English course."

JERK

We have here a vertical look in depth of a soda jerk, arkatypical American. He is a guy who sweats it out in this chain drug store and relates non-threateningly but meaningly to customers and passersby and to all the paperbacks by guys like Neechie, Kant, Marx, O'Neal and Sinclairs— Upton and Lewis. What we have here of course is classic bartender-priest-father symbol, but translated into hard-hitting human comedy terms. Couple titles: Egg Cream, Cupajoe, A Bromo for All Time, Fry One-Bleed It.

Rugged, he thought, very rugged, as he wrote "Nice feel here, good universality, but . . . welllll? Hang in there, fella." He stared out at 51st Street and wondered if he could have been wrong after all. Maybe . . . No. Time, give it time. But . . . No, dammit, time . . . He got up and walked past Sally and said, "Through for the day, honey; anyone wants me, I'm at Toots's."

The bar was filling up rapidly and he wedged in between the man from *Viewpoint* and a *Look* photographer.

"Regular, Charlie," he said. "So dry I've got to inhale it."

"Check, Mr. Mac," Charlie said, bending, mixing, shaking, pouring. "Tough day?"

"Tough." Tasting and nodding, he breathed deeply and turned to *Viewpoint*. "When're you coming to work for me, Paul?" he said.

"For you, anytime. For that little vulture you slave for, never." *Viewpoint* threw down a drink and smiled at him. "Never."

"Oh, come on," MacBean said, vaguely annoyed. "He's only trying to do a job. He's got to cut it close; you know we can't compete in the marketplace."

"I know."

"He's not running for mayor."

Viewpoint held up a hand. "Hey, he's *your* problem. So what else is new?"

Laughing, MacBean dug into the peanuts and scanned the house. A thin presence pushed in between him and the *Look* man and he inched over. "Place is full of action today," he said, and *Viewpoint* looked around and nodded.

"Here's where I really wanna work," he said, "if Toots'll only have me."

MacBean felt a tap on his shoulder and inched over some more as he said, "You'd never make it, Paul." He thought of *Jerk* and looked at Charlie. "You," he said thoughtfully, "do not have Charlie's detached relatedness." Again he felt the tap and this time he turned to the thin presence. He overshot the head, dropped his eyes and looked into the serious-shy face of Harry Braxton, who cleared his throat and said, "Excuse me, Mr. Mac-Bean . . ."

". . . See, see," said *Viewpoint,* "your goddam education is showing again. Does Nelsma know you read a book?"

"He knows." He made room for Harry, who was holding a beer, but not drinking. "Hi Harry," he said, "I've never seen you here." His file card flashed: "One flop academic novel. One beautiful section, two excellent bits. Whole doesn't hang. History major, psych minor. May be in over his head, but needs outside world to produce . . ."

"I thought you might be here," Braxton said. "I took a chance. I left a little early."

"That's okay, Harry."

"Well, I took a chance. I wouldn't ordinarily. I'd like to talk to you about Benedict Arnold."

Viewpoint was nudging him. "Isn't that Gloria Vanderbilt over there? With the hair?"

"Hell no," he said. "That's Cindy Kretzer, from Seldon-Loughlin. The whole conformation's different. What're you drinking, boy? What did you say, Harry? Arnold Bennett?"

"Benedict Arnold."

"I like that," said *Viewpoint.* "In my heart of hearts, I've always yearned for Gloria Vanderbilt. I've always felt she had so much more than just money."

"Benedict Arnold, Mr. MacBean."

"I tell you," MacBean said, "there's no connection. They're two utterly different types. Physically. Emotionally. Background-wise. What about Benedict Arnold, Harry?"

"Well, I think," Harry said, "he'd be right for a series. He's very interesting . . ."

"What, Harry?"

"Hey, Mac," *Viewpoint* said, "I'm gonna move in. You care to join me? She's got a friend."

"No thanks, I've got to shove soon. You were saying, Harry . . ."

"He's a very interesting character. Developmentally. And his contemporaries and his times have not, to my knowledge, been explored on the television."

He winced; you went to *the* Allegheny College, Harry? *Viewpoint* was nudging again. "No, go ahead, Paul," he said. "Good luck. Er . . . Harry, I, er . . ." The heat, the noise, the extra-dries were closing in, but he fought them off, reached out, clamped onto Benedict Arnold and began to posthole: Saratoga. Whomp! West Point. Whomp! Washington. Whomp! Philadelphia. Whomp! Peggy, Drive, Energy, Greed, Success, Despair . . . Whomp, Whomp, Whomp, Whomp, Whomp, WHOMP . . . He saw *Viewpoint* walking away, saw him sit down beside Cindy, saw him smile and begin the pitch. But all around him now the action had become video, no audio; the arc in his mind had closed and he realized the thing had happened, just as the little sonuvagun knew it would. Grayson MacBean could *indeed* bridge the gap.

He gazed down at Harry. "Harry baby," he said, "give me an intensive treatment. Overview. Direction. Slant. The works. Get under his skin. Slide around in there. *Beaucoup* empathy. You can do it, Harry baby."

"Thank you, Mr. MacBean. I know I can."

3

"All right," said P. Nelsma, "convince me."

"This," said MacBean, pacing in front of the great desk, "is really in the American grain. Top general, brilliant man, confidant of Washington. Gorgeous wife. The beautiful American curve. Ascent, triumph, the thrust to the top. It permeates our culture."

"I'll buy that. So?"

"*Whoosh.*" Plummeting into a leather chair, MacBean crumpled up and clutched his stomach. He peeked over the arm. "*Alles kaput.*"

"Zero?"

"*Minus* zero."

"Mmmmmm." P. Nelsma stared, swiveled, stared. "The old snapper." His eyes were thoughtful.

"Complete. Unadulterated."

"Mmmmm," said P. Nelsma. He bounced up and poised against a bookcase. "O. Henry . . . I don't know if it'll play today."

"Nels, listen—"

"Excuse me," said Harry Braxton from a corner of the red leather sofa. He sat up knife straight. "Mr. Nelsma, Benedict Arnold was a very complex man."

"Yes?"

"A very complex, very sensitive man. This would not be a one-dimensional series, Mr. Nelsma."

"I'm listening," said P. Nelsma. "That's part of my secret. I listen."

"That's *it*, Nels," said MacBean. "Braxton has identified our point of attack. It would be a genuine portrait in depth. With every wart and wen thrown in. The sweet and the sour. It's ultramodern."

"Mmmm," said P. Nelsma from his stool. He shook out his built-in creases, leaned an elbow carefully against one, leaned his chin carefully against his hand. "Dick Whitney, king of the hill, sells out from the top of the stock exchange. Hell of an O. Henry bit there . . ."

"Sure Nels." MacBean began pacing again. "Look, why stop with Arnold? *All* the players for great stakes. Aaron Burr . . ."

"Maximilian in Mexico," said Harry Braxton.

"How about Bill Bryan?" said P. Nelsma. "He got a ter-*rif*ic shafting from Darrow."

"And *four* times an unsuccessful candidate," said Harry Braxton.

"Go go," muttered P. Nelsma. "Nicky of Russia."

"Of course," said MacBean. "Laval."

"Yeah."

"Pétain," said Harry Braxton.

"Yeah."

"Hell," said MacBean, "Adolf."

P. Nelsma slid down his stool and began to pace. "Don't say a single goddam thing," he said, closing his eyes and picking his way skillfully across the carpet. After three trips he stopped and with his eyes still closed said, "Okay, devil-advocate it." He threw his head back and opened his mouth. "Ahhh, it's downbeat." His head came down and he smiled. "Hell, it's loaded with identification. Every schnook who ever failed." Head up. "War is hump . . . Nuts, a good story line has the eternal values . . . Okay okay . . . It's too real." Smile. "Hell, it's not *that* real." Harry smiled too. P.

Nelsma opened his eyes, leaped for his desk and slid across the top, his old socko boffo finale. Stopping a delicate inch from the edge, he said, "One-note . . . It is one-note." He raised his arms, closed his eyes again and monotoned, "Burr, Bryan, Laval, Adolf, Nicky . . . Shoeless Joe Jackson, Jesus Christ, Jesus *Christ*. Wow! We've got a whole vertical concept. A Sunday nightful. A night for losers. *Losers*. See?" The eyes popped open. "Okay, Mac, Braxton, I wanna pilot. *The Benedict Arnold Show*. It'll be strictly an Apex baby, no movie outfit muscles in. Hey, and listen, we go live. Yowsa. I'll sell the board, leave it to me. Three segments, I want three, we'll reset our whole Sunday night format, it's from hunger anyway. Any questions?"

"Mr. Nelsma," said Harry Braxton.

"Yes, Harry?"

"I have this idea for a spin-off on Major John André."

"Now hear this . . . opus number four:

Media popular, media mass,
need be myopular? got to be crass?
A flatuland, wasteland, where truth never festers?
Read bland-hearted Hazels for tragic prim Hesters?
Not with a boss who proves catalytic,
whose notions are boffo, if not analytic,
So bring on the Point and old Saratoga,
CBS lost Berra
and we've got the Yoga!"

4

For Arnold they got Vic Fusari, for Peggy, Joy Krinlein, who left an eight-month run in *Charcoal and Dust*. On a Friday afternoon, Manny Winkle, the old soft-shoe man who had made a string of thirties musicals with Nelsma, fought his way into the office and convinced everyone he was Washington.

During this time Harry Braxton spent a week in Philadelphia and another week in Saratoga and two days in New Haven (for Captain Arnold) and when he returned holed up in the Writers Wrest on the fourteenth floor where in eight days he turned out three scripts. With the scripts, MacBean, Vic, Joy, Harry and Manny, P. Nelsma walked into Milton Lawitz's apartment on West Fourth Street and talked him out of another season of repertory and into fifteen segments of *The Benedict Arnold Show*. Milton was pacing through his apartment and quivering when they left.

After a week of rehearsal, which Milton insisted upon, and MacBean supported, they ran through the three segments chronologically ("the only way I work"), exciting Milton so much that he demanded a fourth, at which point P. Nelsma said the hell with budgets, when you catch lightning in a bottle, go go go, and sent Harry back to the Wrest, where he whirled off two more scripts.

Then, with Arnold dashing impatiently up the success ladder, pausing, interlocking poignantly with Peggy, P. Nelsma planted a few soft leads at Shor's, the Downtown AC, the Stadium Club and in four columns, and from nineteen bidders allowed Gomper's denture paste, Mulleavey's WarBang toys and Instant Drop insect bomb to sponsor the show.

5

The Benedict Arnold Show received three raves from the morning papers and two from the evening. The only dissenter, supplying what P. Nelsma called the controversial clincher, was George Wastung in *NewsReview,* who had spent eight months in the RAF supply center in 1940, and questioned the advisability of reopening old wounds at a time like this.

Benny jumped immediately into the top twenty at Arbitron. Two magazines saluted it as show of the month, another called it top-drawer family entertainment and clean clean clean! In three weeks it was top ten in all three surveys, neck and neck with *Back Bay Moonshiners* and *Doc Digby.*

It seemed that everyone connected with *Benny* caught fire. Vic Fusari proved conclusively that he could do something besides brood. Joy revealed a new softness, was all army wives in one. Manny began a brand new career as a creator of historical portraits. And Milton . . . Milton demonstrated with exquisite sensitivity and perception that, in the words of opus number five, "Hark Hark the Lark could sell *and* could spark."

And behind it all, building the smooth, driving power that moved them all, was Harry Braxton and his dedication. His story line was jagged when it had to be, subtle where it had to be, tough and tender (always) and terribly rich in human-interest values, heartbreaking in its accumulation of identification grabbers. With each new script MacBean found himself squirming in anticipation as he climbed with Arnold toward the summit and dreaded and loved every step of the way.

Each Monday Harry would walk into his office with an outline for the next inevitable jump. They would chat, Mac-Bean would quietly marvel, Harry would smile shyly and walk out and on Friday deliver the finely wrought chapter that pushed *Benny* closer to the precipice.

On the Monday after they returned from West Point, where they had shot some background footage, MacBean was busy at his workbench in the corner of his office. It had been a trying weekend. He had spent the entire night pacing the Hudson with Vic, who was beginning to tense up with overinvolvement.

"Christ," he kept saying, pounding his palm as they walked, "I don't think I can sell out, I really don't."

And MacBean kept gentling him down.

"Vic baby," he said over and over again, softly, insistently, "you are an*ti*cipating and dammit you *know* better. What would Strasberg say?"

Vic, pounding, muttering, "Yeah, yeah I know it, I jam it down, but then . . . I can't *help* it, man."

Until at four in the morning he maneuvered him back to the Thayer, fed him a Seconal, tucked him in and rushed back to town. And so the Monday morning workbench, to work off the tension and, more important, to postpone the tragedy with small, tangible basics.

He was working on a lamp base when he heard Harry's apologetic knock. Washing hands and face quickly, he slid into his jacket, hurried to his desk, shuffled papers and yelled come on in, Harry. Harry slipped in neatly, clutching his cardboard briefer.

"Morning, Mr. MacBean," he said, drawing pages out of the briefer. He placed them gently on the desk.

"Hi Harry, sit," MacBean said. "How goes it?"

"Very well, Mr. MacBean."

"How was the weekend? I didn't see very much of you at the Point."

"Fine, Mr. MacBean. I did two installments."

"Uh huh. Say Harry, I don't think I ever really told you how I feel about this thing you've created . . ."

"I didn't really create it, Mr. MacBean."

"No, of course not. I mean, the way you molded it into an artistic unity."

"The deterministic forces inside and outside of Arnold really molded . . ."

"Sure, sure, Harry. Of course. Well, anyway, I wanted you to know. Okay, let's see what you've got." He picked up the outline, spun around smartly and glanced down Madison Avenue and began to read. He read it once quickly, looked up and sighted down Madison, then read again, slowly. Then again, quickly. And looked up again. He couldn't be sure, but . . . again to the script . . . come on now . . . He swiveled around. "Harry," he said softly, spacing his words, "what the hell do you mean you're changing the ending?"

"Well, Mr. MacBean," Harry said, "I think the deterministic forces call for it."

"Harry," still quiet, still spacing, "what do you mean you think?"

"Well, it's my professional judgment . . ."

"Oh?" MacBean got up and walked to his workbench and rubbed his hands over the lamp base. "Your judgment. What about *history,* Harry?" he asked gently. The lamp base was rough and soothing.

"Frankly, I think history was wrong in this case," Harry said.

"How was that, Harry?"

"I've thoroughly analyzed all the social and psychological factors, all the centrifugal and centripetal forces at work here, and everything adds up irrevocably to a heroic denouement for Arnold."

The lamp base slid a splinter into his thumb. "Hey, Harry fella, you know what you're saying?"

"Look, Mr. MacBean." Harry was tipped on the edge of the sofa. "Look," he said, "at how lousy you've been feeling the past week. You know why, don't you?"

"Naturally. I think about this guy—"

"And the whole company, look how upset they are."

"Sure. We're involved. Hell, it's a tribute to *you,* Harry."

"Two million people are upset."

"Sure Harry. God, Harry, I'd give my right arm if Arnold didn't fink."

"See? You said didn't, not hadn't. Two million viewers feel the same way." He smiled. "That is a psychohistorical determinant."

"What, Harry?"

"I worked it all out, Mr. MacBean."

"You worked it out, Harry?"

"Mr. MacBean, I would like to ask you something. Tell me, how do you feel about Booth shooting Lincoln?"

He tried to force his hand through the lamp base. "Oh God, God, Harry, if only he'd misfired, if only that damn guard—"

"See?" Harry said. He stood and walked to the door and looked back. "Think it over, Mr. MacBean."

He ran through a dozen sheets of sandpaper, shellacked the lamp base, slashed out a design for an end table, powered through the top, cut it to pieces, jigsawed a half-dozen happy profiles, half-dozen sad profiles, hacked them to pieces, swept the workbench clean, took a hot shower and walked down the hall to P. Nelsma's office. When he reached the great desk, Harry Braxton was perched on the red leather chair beside it.

"Hiya Mac," said P. Nelsma, swiveling and braking with a tiny foot. "Sitsee. Harry and I were just kicking the gong around."

He slid onto a high stool and smiled at Harry, smiled at P. Nelsma. "Nels," he said, folding his arms, "I guess you're aware that we've got ourselves a bit of a problem."

Far down, Madison Avenue was beginning to jam with the going-home and fast-drink crowd; he focused on straw hats coming out of *Look.*

"Well, in a way," said P. Nelsma. "Harry filled me in. You, I gather, are not so happy, are you, Mac?"

Eight straws, one panama; so they *were* coming back. He unfolded. "Oh, it's not quite *that,* Nels," he said. "Hell, what I feel personally isn't important."

"But of course it is, Mac."

"Well, what I mean is, Harry's done such a damn fine

job that I want to be sure *he's* not hurt. You know, by the way we handle this.''

"Uh huh."

The uptown buses were filling. "Sometimes," Mac-Bean said reasonably, "we become enmeshed in a problem. We lose a little perspective. Hell, Fusari's almost *sick* with the idea of giving away West Point."

"Kid's really involved, huh?"

"You know it. So I'd like Harry to feel absolutely secure about this. To know that we still want him and appreciate him. We *both* want and appreciate him. And, well, he works so damn fast he can still pull it out by Friday."

P. Nelsma tilted far back; his eyes picked at the ceiling; he drummed on his chin. "I like Harry's bit," he said.

MacBean folded his arms and smiled wider. The hurry-home girls were stepping to the rear of the buses. "Nels," he said gently, "it's not just a bit. That's the point. Harry is tampering with history. We can't do that type of thing."

"You preaching to me, Kenyon?"

"Nels, you know better. You know what I think of you." He slid down the stool and sat on the desk. "But, I've got to do my job. We simply have to get our focus straight, that's all. After all, we *do* have a responsibility. This isn't show business."

"Harry," P. Nelsma said to the ceiling, "historical determinism make psychological sense?"

"Absolutely, Mr. Nelsma," Harry said.

"Motivation? Cause? Effect? Sensible story line?"

"Completely."

"So," P. Nelsma said, dipping down. "There's your *show* business. May I remind you that *Louis Pasteur* pulled in an Oscar *and* made a mint."

"Hey, Nels, you're not serious? Nobody *tampered* with Louis Pasteur . . ."

"Why should they? He was a hero. Suppose he'd sold *out.* You think he'd get an Oscar?"

MacBean stared at Madison Avenue. Two, three, four buses were moving in line; lousy transportation. All the packed-in office girls. Pouring out in the seventies, stopping off for groceries, clacking up four flights. Flicking the on-off button. He stood up. "Wait a minute. Wait a minute. What's going on here? You really think you can sell this? You think those people down there are idiots?"

P. Nelsma gazed at him. "I sell," he shrugged. "They buy."

MacBean reached for the back of his head, slid down and kneaded his tight, tense neck. "What about O. Henry?" he said.

"Harry? . . ." said P. Nelsma.

"O. Henry really wasn't psychologically valid," said Harry.

"Hell," said P. Nelsma, "this out-Henrys O. Henry. A *double* snapper." He flicked a hand. "Go ahead, go ahead, devil me."

"What about the loser concept?" MacBean said.

"The real grabber. Every loser out there becomes a *winner.* It's so goddam simple it took a loser like Harry to come up with it." Harry smiled modestly.

"Mr. Nelsma," MacBean said, "Benedict Arnold was a traitor to this country. He was not, repeat *not,* a hero. The American public knows that."

"Mr. Kenyon," said P. Nelsma, "lemme tell you something, okay? I was in three-D. Remember? Yowsa, right in on the ground floor; I had a very sizable piece of the action. Well, the American public came into the theater, see, and just begged for this wild set of cardboard glasses and sat down there with these nutty things on, and the American public was in heaven. We could have draped a toilet seat around their necks . . .''

"Goddammit, three-D folded up!"

"Because *we* didn't have the guts to give em bigger and better *toilet seats.*"

MacBean looked at the buses. It was so friendly in those buses. "The FCC," he said finally.

"Come on, buster. With all the loot our sponsors got tied up in this? Oh brother."

"All right," MacBean said quietly. "Let this alone for a minute. Where do we go from here?"

"Hell, Harry's got some *great* things on tap. Robert E. Lee, Kaiser Wilhelm . . ."

"Whoa," said MacBean. "Lee, well at least Lee is a genuine folk hero, but the Kaiser? You're going to switch on *him?*"

"Heynow, Mr. Ideals," P. Nelsma grinned. He waggled a finger and looked at him sideways. "What's the substantive difference, hah Mac baby?" He winked. "And we've got to be impartial. This determinism thing has to have depth and breadth and variety. That's why it's great; it's so goddam ap*ply*-able."

"I . . . ah . . ."

"See?"

"I . . ."

"Sure, Mac."

"Ah . . . I . . . have to think about this . . ."

"Sure."

"I think I'll knock off. It's been a . . . peculiar day."

"Sure. After all, Harry's *your* boy, isn't he?"

"Well . . ."

P. Nelsma walked around his desk, took MacBean's arm and escorted him to the door. "Let me do the worrying, okay Mac? That's what they're paying me for. Forcryinoutloud, they're only shadows on a piece of glass; what's the big deal? Right? Right. Oh, and Mac."

"Yes?"

"Mac, please don't get cute."

"Cute?"

"Uh huh. Harry."

Harry reached down and dug a finger into the desk. Filling the room was a vaguely familiar voice; that is, it should have been familiar except it was Donald Duck's voice. And Donald was saying peculiar, familiar things. *CBSlostBerra,* shrilled Donald, *andwe'vegottheYoga.* Harry punched again and Donald quacked again, *mediapopularmediamass* . . . Harry kept punching; Donald kept quacking.

"Hey, Louie Carroll," said P. Nelsma, slicing the air and silencing Donald. "You gonna write one of those inside exposés? A satirical novel? Life in the bagel factory? Are you, baby? Hell, you like the kinda loot this gig pays, don't you, baby? And all the fringe benefits. You don't *really* object to being a member of this industry? You read me?"

6

In two days he had dug out the hull of Old Ironsides, molded the forecastle and penciled in riggings. Beneath his sketch, over and over, he wrote, "Ay, tear her tattered ensign down, long has she waved on high."

On Friday, as he glued on the mainmast the script came back to him with *appr P. Nelsma* scribbled above the title. Under the title, which was "Drums to Glory," was written, "Dear Mac, just read this; give it—all of us—a chance, willyahuh?"

So he read. In the corner of his office, beside Old Ironsides. And it was a beautiful thing. Simple, plastic, filled with the terror and magnificence and reality of those years, humane, direct. Fair. And it was just as valid when he read it behind his desk. And still as right at lunch, at a side table at Shor's.

After lunch he walked to Fifth and continued up to the park, past the Fighting Doughboys, driving, falling, dying as they pushed over the top. There on a bench, with the stone boys behind him, imploring him to keep faith, he felt the power of historical determinism. It poured out of those magnificent helmets, down the tough old Enfields, out along the bayonets, and it righted all the wrongs, cleaned up the doubts, cleared out no-man's-land . . .

It was after three when he got back to the office. Still standing, he wrote a note to P. Nelsma asking if he could hold the script for a while. The answer bounced back, "Sure thing, no rush atall." He slipped it into his briefer and left at three-thirty, walking slowly downtown to 33rd and then east to First. All evening he was very quiet with Maggie. Before he went to bed he read it once more and cried for the first time since Roosevelt died.

The next morning he sent the script back to P. Nelsma. On the stapled interoffice that said FROM THE DESK OF GRAYSON MACBEAN, he wrote "Now they can bury the poor bastard with his leg."

P. Nelsma walked into his office, held out his hand and said, "Thanks, Mac, that's beautiful."

A gigantic wave of relief rolled over the company. By the end of the week they had all folded securely into "Drums to Glory," Vic, especially, showing a new, humble strength, as if he had discovered a new dimension in himself. Mac-Bean sat with him till 3:30 in the morning at P.J.'s, while he explained what this meant to his career. And on Sunday they shared a good-luck drink in his office before Vic went across town for the show. As he left, Vic hook-shot his Amytals into the wastebasket.

Alone, MacBean puttered around Ironsides and tried a few sketches of the Battery Fort. Then he glanced at the clock, closed up shop and walked downstairs. He walked along Central Park South, past Simón Bolívar, past "Remember the *Maine*." He walked slowly, backed up by the gallant sailors, "By fate unwarned, in death unafraid." There at the entrance to the park the spinning wheel of determinism circled around the hub of Columbus Circle, uprooting steel, concrete and Huntington Hartford, and exposed tier on miserable tier of history gone wrong. And righted the wrong:

Lindy haranguing the motley crew at the Garden? Hell. He flashes an FBI card and pinches Fritz Kuhn . . .

Christy Mathewson shriveling to nothing inside the glorious pin stripes, eh? Why, Trudeau grabs him and farms him out to Saranac Lake and he's back in '19, mowing down the hated Cubs . . .

The draft riots. Yes, those horrible panics rippling easily through this wonderful town. Oh? Wasn't that, yes, it was, Jeff Davis, original Commie provocateur . . .

Hendrik Hudson? The double snapper. Climbs with junior back onto the *Half Moon,* puts down the misguided mutineers (forgives), sails to glory, settles down on . . . West Point . . . the Point . . .

He sat down breathlessly on a bench beneath the *Maine,* gazed west and then upriver, to where Patton and Blackjack stood guard over the mothball fleet and all the gallant young Douglas Macs. Of course. The Point was still there, wasn't it? Turning out the stars. Didn't that prove it? That determinism worked. That it made beautiful, irrevocable sense despite the miserable history books? *Didn't* it?

Georgie Patton's varnished helmet swiveled slowly in the Hudson sunset. Blackjack's tough, ramrod neck bristled out of the iron collar. The mothball fleet shuddered. Wasn't *any* body buying? Wait. How about the thousands of shavetails carved out of the long gray line, sleeping in San Juan, Thierry, Iwo and Bastogne? Wouldn't *they* take care of one of their own? Hell, he had to smile.

He pulled back to Huntington Hartford and the frightful, dependable Coliseum and he looked up at the *Maine* sailor boys. Okay, Lindy *had* taken the medal from Goering. Yes, Big Six *had* gone west, at ninety pounds. All right, cowards, thousands of cowards stampeded the city, and yes, yes, Hendrik had drifted forever into the night . . . The shavetails knew; Georgie and Blackjack knew . . . Don't get cute, eh? You like this gig, fella? "Dammit," he muttered, "they bled and they died." He stood up and squared his shoulders. "And they gave us our pride."

Vic was leaning against a wall with his eyes closed and his lips moving in violent preparation. Joy was knitting and Milton was shuffling in place and blinking. P. Nelsma was sitting behind control, as usual, and he waved as MacBean walked in. MacBean waved back and stood behind Sal Barbio on number one camera. At twenty seconds before prime time, Milton took a noisy breath, walked behind Sal, held up a hand and shouted *"Silencio."* MacBean closed his eyes and saw the millions, glued to sets and horse-collared with toilet seats. And the words flashed, running across his forehead like bulletins on the *Times* building: he saw them so clearly: *How do you do. My name is Grayson MacBean and I am the executive producer of this show. I am also the first vice-president of this network, which means I am in a position of responsibility, much responsibility. Therefore, I must tell each and every one of you that the show you are about to see, this episode, is a complete, calculated fraud. Therefore,* **The Benedict Arnold Show** *is a fraud. What you are about to see, my friends, and I've never felt so close to you as I do now, is a cynical attempt to deceive you. To play on your notorious gullibility. Now it is just possible that this is so, that you sit there stupefied, that you do not care. That, of course, is possible, but I choose not to believe it. I don't* want *to believe it. But even so, even if this is true, I must tell you that* I *know what is about to happen, that I bear a prime responsibility. Therefore, I ask you to* watch, *yes to watch, and then with calls, telegrams, with all your great, untapped power, rise up and tell this network, yes and its supervisors, just what you think of it. For, ladies and gentlemen, if* *you're the kind of folks I think you are, am* hoping *you are, you will then keep the faith with Patton, Pershing, Lieutenant Douglas Mac—*

The distant sound of drums invaded the *Times* building and cracked against his forehead. He opened his eyes. Across the gray barracks, above the cliffs, P. Nelsma sat behind the glass, gazing proudly down. Beside him sat Harry Braxton, prim and stiff, with his set little smile. And beside Harry, Gibby, Istvan and Marty. At that moment P. Nelsma looked at the four writers and at MacBean and nodded and gave him thumbs up.

MacBean looked away, then up at the writers straining forward, absorbing the very first success. Success? *How do you do, my name is* . . . He looked at the four already savoring the next moment . . . *I am also the first vice-president of this network, which means* . . . The four of them, the big four, learning their lessons . . . *Therefore, I must tell each and every one of you, I must* . . . His team, his stable . . . *With all your great untapped* . . . His breakthrough. Christ . . . *great untapped* . . . Christ . . . power.

He took a tremendous breath, let it out and, ignoring the funny little guy behind the glass, he smiled on his boys and then turned to A GRAYSON MACBEAN PRODUCTION, *THE BENEDICT ARNOLD SHOW.*

SIMON
GIRTY
GO APE

The sun. It shafted in a thin, revolving tube of dust and gloom, revealing her profile in a moment of such complete involvement that for the first time in the afternoon Leonard relaxed and marked up a plus in his battle against Radio City Music Hall. He was moved even to touch her hair as she bent over the case of wampum and headbands. But the action, as if he were rearranging a private connection, broke her delicate concentration, and she looked up with a smile divided equally into complaisance and pout. Encouraged, but still cautious, Leonard stepped to the case, draped his arm lightly over her shoulder and let his voice trail over the finance and fashion of middle-class Algonquins with a slow, impressed y-e-a-hhhh . . .

She nodded. "That one," Sylvia said, all seriousness, bending over a green, blue, orange braid, "that's a lovely headache band and it just goes with . . ." she pointed to a swath of green, blue, orange wampum ". . . that."

Leonard felt his second wave of encouragement. "Why that's right, honey. I hadn't even noticed," he enthused. "The money and the merchandise *match*. Gee here you are being natural and spontaneous and the old professor doesn't even see the trees for the forest." His arm slipped to her tiny, tight middle, made to measure for the wampum belt. Before he could catch himself, he had kissed her.

"Leonard please." She smoothed her sweater and pulled it down as if he had reached inside. "We're in a public place." She moved away. Primly. To the center aisle, where a full-sized Iroquois squaw, dressed in fringed buckskin, frozen in full, purposeful stride, stopped her retreat. From the wampum case Leonard watched as the eyes of the two maidens met, gripped, and understood the problem of overeager bucks. He tiptoed to within a carefully measured sunbeam-tube, and, grinning stupidly, prepared for total apology. "Oh, Leonard," she said with a childlike delight that swept away his elaborate defense-system, "she's real, she's just perfectly real."

"Of course, honey," he said quickly, marveling at his good fortune. "That's the whole point. All this . . ." He swept the room, stocked with tension, drive, life—protected by a fat, dozing guard, mummified by three museum-girls with notebooks, appraised by two giggling boys—"All of it," he said, "really functioned and experienced. Love, hate, fear, compulsive drive, all the things we feel . . ."

"She looks just like Suzy Parker. The high cheekbones and all."

"Sure, honey," he said, blocking the sigh. "She could have been the Suzy of her tribe. That's precisely the point." His hand was rewarded with a squeeze and he gazed gratefully into Suzy's empty, exquisitely mascaraed eyes.

". . . And just look at that darling papoose," Sylvia said. She reached over and (ignoring museum regulations) stroked the fat, pink cheeks that poked up over the squaw's shoulder. "He's just like a Baby Dear. Oh Leonard, Suzy has a baby, too."

"Well . . ." The urge to sweep her up blended with annoyance. "Well . . . Suzy could learn a thing or two from this one . . ." (Hmmm, Suzy, striding, hatbox in hand, from one assignment to another, while the rosy cheeks paled in a nursery . . . Hmmm . . .) "You see," he said, crinkling his forehead, "there is a genuine mechanism of nature at work here, a real physicality that the baby shares with the mother. Practically always. A real love-warmth. And incidentally, this provides the mother with a deeply satisfying relationship. A . . . circle of love, as it were." He waited anxiously; Sylvia's hand stroked the tiny head, massaged the dangling feet. A discreet cough from the guard shot her hand to her hair. "Oh yes," she said, hands fluttering. "I see what you mean." And Leonard, allying himself with childlike spontaneity against official coughers, gently circled her middle and said, "Now Sylvia, aren't you really glad you came? Honest injun now? Isn't this more satisfying than Radio City?"

"Well it is nicer than I *thought.*" Serious look, replacing natural spontaneity. "Yes," she finally decided, leaning against him. "I *am* glad you brought me, Leonard. You certainly know the kookiest out-of-the-way-places." He leaned toward her and momentarily lost his balance as she ducked away. Coughs, tie-straightening, smile; he watched her clack off in those incredible heels. His shoulders sagged, then stiffened. She had stopped before the weapons case, filled with hard, flinted hate; she was caught in the Radio City version of circling Indians and doomed settlers and once again the subtle annoyance-tenderness blend filled him, wagged his head as it misted his eyes. He felt a light jostle and stepped aside as the two giggling boys squeezed in between him and the case of the Plains Indian. One of the boys, short, pale, with erupting skin and long, damp hair, kept digging the other with his elbow. "Hey Chief Joseph. How bout that. You a *chief.*" The other boy, equally small and thin, was a very dark Negro. He seemed rooted to the floor by tremendous, oversized workshoes. He stuck three fingers behind his head, waggled them and doubled over. Smiling and shaking his head, Leonard stepped carefully around them and walked to Sylvia. The boys, unkempt, unaware, had reinforced him. Like a concerned parent, he watched as Sylvia, now done with bows, arrows and doomed settlers, chose from the allure of the Hopi, the reason of the Ojibwa, the romance of the Blackfoot. Ahhh the scholar should have known. Pocahontas. A

smile, a frown, the spank-kiss impulse. He settled for
crossed arms and a quizzical expression. Well why not? The
light brown doll beneath them, beautifully made up, was
sprawling daintily over the husky, bearded captain, his
head on the chopping block, twisted up and grinning
smugly at Powhatan. Drama, conflict, rivalry. Life. Yes, but
. . . for an instant he longed for the purity of the giggling
boys, uncluttered by Technicolored history. Then Sylvia
looked up at him, her eyes brimming with potential. He
nodded encouragingly.

"I remember her," she said, her voice soft with respect. "I remember that exact same picture in my Six-B
History." Leonard nodded. "I always loved her," she said.
"The way she stood up to her father and all." He reached
over and brushed her cheek; she pressed his hand against
her face; his heart sprinted . . .

"Chief Jo-siph. Oh Chiffy wiffy." The acne king
minced by on tiptoes and bowed. Before him stood the
ball-and-chain-shoes, his arms folded proudly. "You dere,"
said the ball and chain, "you Ossie. Osceola. Boy, you gotta
clean up them swamps. Get ridda all them muhskeetuhs.
That's my order, Ossie boy." Osceola bowed deeply and
broke down with giggles. The Chief, losing his regal com-
posure, gasped for air. The two of them shook silently,
framing Leonard and Sylvia as if neither of them existed.
Sylvia's eyes popped open and her nose crinkled as she
caught the upwind scent of sweat and dirty hair. She stared
at Leonard; he smiled and nodded reassuringly. Then as if
neither of them had yet materialized, the two boys recov-
ered and clattered away. Sylvia's head swiveled. "Rude
things." she said sternly. Leonard patted her cheek. "Well
honey, they're just being terribly involved. Actually they're
responding very naturally. On their terms of course." Her

eyes flipped up, then down. "Oh, they didn't even *look* at this case. If they're so involved you'd think they'd look at least. An Indian princess saves the white captain in spite of her father, and then they get married . . ."

"She didn't marry John Smith," he said quickly.

"She didn't?"

"No, she married John Rolfe, a planter from Virginia. She changed her name to Rebecca."

"Rebecca Rolfe."

"Uh huh. She even went to England with him. But she didn't adjust very well to her new environment. She died quite young."

"Oh."

"She uhhh just wasn't suited . . ."

"She knew she should have married John *Smith,* that's why. He was a lot cuter anyway."

"Now honey . . ."

"Her *father* probably broke it up. Oh you're so smart." Her perfume and soap filled the space out of which she had swished. He turned, head shaking, and followed, equating Smith with all the smug, Vandyked connivers in history. Probably scoring heavily in the Virginia evenings as cuckolded Rolfe cured his tobacco. He sighed and settled gently beside her and scrutinized Algonquin artifacts, firmly sealing off Jamestown in his history-of-the-mind.

"Just look at that workmanship," he said, pointing at a tarnished spoon. "It's very nearly twentieth-century in feeling and control." Sylvia hunched away from him. "Say," he continued—brightly—"how about that rattle? Look at that finger grip. The beads." He perceived a loosening around her shoulders. "Why it's just perfect for tiny little fingers." She leaned forward and smiled. "Maybe," he continued, "that nice little guy back there played with it once." Her sigh cut through him. "Oh, Leonard," she said, "Oh, it's so sad."

"What? Why, sweetie?"

"That darling little baby. He'll never *really* play with the rattle."

"Well no, I guess not. Not *really* . . ."

"He's dead, Leonard."

He reached for this little girl and held her. For an instant the bulging softness relaxed against him; he flooded with protectiveness. Then she was free. But smiling. "You're sweet," she said. Her head tossed downwind. "Not like those." He looked at the gigglers in the next aisle and felt terribly clean, sensitive and . . . He squashed the sensation and said, "Now Sylvie, they have a few problems I don't have. You know?" She patted his cheek, linked his (clean sensitive) arm and pulled him across the hall. He resisted gently, feeling that somehow he still hadn't done enough for them. For her, really. "Wait honey," he said. "Just a sec." She stopped, frowned and took a deep breath. "Hold it, sweetie." He guided her along the aisle to a case opposite the boys. "Don't let them see," he whispered.

"Oh Leonard."

"Just one minute."

The boys were standing before "The Indian and the White Man," for once without the standard giggle. The little Negro, all thought and evaluation, stuck a finger against the placard and read slowly: "Si-mon Gir-ty. Ren-a-gade. Si-mon Gir-ty, at the age of thirty-seven, lef his village an went to live with a nearby tribe. He marry an Indian girl an . . . fought against the white settlers . . ." They both stepped closer and studied the crude painting of Girty, hair braided, mouth twisted with disgust as he viewed the white man's world. "Hey, Phillip," said the reader, "this cat pack it in an go ape." The white boy nodded. "Yeah, he cut right out." His hand peeled away from the village. "Zoom." They nodded and stood quietly, respectfully. Leonard stiffened, finger on his lips. Then he felt the tug. "Leonard, will you come on." A tongue of anger flared and was instantly crushed. "Sure sure, honey. In a minute," he said, holding off her pressure. The boys. They had walked across the aisle, to Manhattan Island, heads bent, absorbing the message of Si-mon Gir-ty, who had been true to himself. So basic, so simple, why in the world hadn't he ever seen that?

"Leonard, let's go upstairs."

"Okay, honey. We'll go. Just wait here a second. Okay?"

Her hand dropped and he heard her lipstick smack. Somehow he would have to make her aware of these little things: lipstick smacks, natural children . . . "Hon, watch these kids. Catch their directness. Hey, look at that . . ." The greatest real estate transaction in history had caught the boys; he held her there for the point he had to make. Important for her to perceive. To know. She Oh deared and he pulled against her resistance until they were directly behind the boys and he had composed them into a larger, more meaningful tableau of his own.

"Leonard please."

"Shhh . . ."

As if on cue, the boys reacted. Heads cocked, they contemplated, assimilated, externalized. Total, enveloping life-style; he squeezed the message into her hand. "Hey Joseph," said the white boy. "You be the white man." Leonard shivered. "See," said the boy, "Peter Minut. An I'm the Indian."

"Ahm allus the white man. Ah wanna be the Indian." The Negro boy pouted; Leonard squeezed Sylvia's arm.

"No, you ain't, Joseph," said the white boy. "*I* was the white man yesterday. Come on Joseph. I change wichou tomorrow."

Leonard's mouth was close to her face. "Hear that," he whispered. "Isn't that just wonderful?" Her head pulled away. "Leonard will you come on. This is just plain silly." He held her tightly, enjoying the pressure. "Okay okay," he nodded. "Yes. No. Wait a minute." Thin, black little Joseph, now the white man, began to slide into his role. One leg stiffened and dragged pitifully after the good one as he circled his opponent. Phillip, the Indian negotiator, ballooned his cheeks, but contained the laughter. "Hey stupid, you Peter *Minut,* not Peter Stuyvesand." The clumper rose and fell in place. "Same difference," he said. "I takes you on one leg." Up down, down up. "Isn't that marvelous?" Leonard murmured. "Will you look at that expression, isn't that priceless? Honey, *look.* Take the scales from your eyes." Her hand flopped in his. "Sylvia, please."

"Okay Chief," said Peter Minuit, his black Dutch face wrinkling with shrewdness, "les make a deal. How much ahm offered for Manhattan?" (Man-a-hattan, Leonard corrected.) The Dutch arm encompassed the island. "Chief, ahm sellin it back to you." Leonard fought down the laughter.

"Ugh Mr. Minut. It ain't much. Cruddy bars, cruddy candy stores, cruddy Polo Grounds, cruddy P.S. Thirty-four."

"Well Chief, you got to look pass all that crud. This place got possibilities. In a thousand years this be a good place to live." Leonard squeezed the lifeless hand.

"Oh you ain't jivin me, Pete. I know *value* when I see it. Les talk turkey. How much you want for these rocks?"

The guard at the table stirred restlessly; Leonard

willed him back into sleepiness. "Leonard." Sylvia's voice was thin and irritable. "Will you please let me know when you're ready." He shook his head. "Do *me* the favor, hon, and listen to what they're saying. What they're *really* saying." The boys were eyeing each other now, the old enemies, equalized on 155th Street and the Broad Way. Man-a-hattan, Haarlem, Leonard, Sylvia, the Museum of the American Indian hung on the Dutchman's reply. Minuit rubbed his face, measuring his responsibility.

"Thirty bucks," he said.

The chief shook his head pityingly. "You kiddin me, Petey? I oney spent ten bucks to get Brooklyn back. You wanna make six bucks on *this* stuff?"

Peter withdrew into his thrifty Dutch soul and clumped thoughtfully in place. The heavyweight shoes groaned as he elevatored and sparred for time. The chief, his acne gleaming with the strain, was an arms-folded triumphant statue. And Sylvia, head to one side, as from a great distance, was finally watching. "Honey," Leonard said, bending to her, "we're giving it back to the *Indians.* Isn't that great?" Her head shook slowly. "How in the world," she whispered, "can you get so excited . . ."

"It's *real,* honey, real. No damn artifice. Oh that little shrewdie. Shhh . . ." The Dutchman had ceased his clumping and suddenly he was reaching behind the chief and over his head; he lifted a belt of wampum off a display. "Now hear this, Chief," he said confidentially, stroking the belt. "See this trinket? It's a regular beauty, ain't it? It sure is. Well ahm throwin it in the pot. Yessir, all this land plus a beeyooteeful bonus giff. Now how bout *that,* Chief?"

The laughter held in Leonard's throat. No, he warned the white Indian, no, don't succumb, don't . . .

"Oh Pete, oh you big Pete," crowed the Chief, solid as

the rock of Man-a-hattan, "you puttin me on. Simon Girty he tol me all about you. Man you bribin me with my own *wampum.*" Leonard exhaled; the small, black, heavy-footed Minuit was confused, scratching his conniving white-man's head. Between them hung the wampum belt, the sweetener that had ruined the transaction. Overconfident exploiter. Leonard chuckled. "Oh that's beautiful, just beautiful. Isn't that priceless?" Oh, if he could only turn impresario and present them in this scene on every street corner from Harlem to Birmingham . . . A blur of T-shirt, a swirl of garlic and the scene had suddenly shattered. The chief, brandishing the belt, was spinning past him, stopping, thumbing his nose at the white man and sprinting away.

"*Crook,*" yelled the startled Peter. Ignoring his infirmity, he shot past Leonard and Sylvia, careened around a corner, past the guard whose *News* fluttered to the floor, and scooted after the Indian thief. Back down the Seminole Corridor fled the chief, waving his victory belt. Past the girls with the notebooks who pressed themselves to the wall and stared in horror. Once more past the guard, who picked up his paper and stared. Past Sylvia who stared. Past Leonard who began to laugh. Quietly at first. Then uncontrollably. *Zoom.* He roared as the chief skidded around the Hopi and accelerated down the straightaway of the Plains Indians, holding his two armslengths over his straining victim. They banked in tandem around another corner and then lost all purpose, and like a pair of waterbugs scooted over the surface with no direction, except where the prize led them. "Hey *crook,*" yelled the black Dutchman, "you dirty crook." The chief roared. "*You the crook,*" he yelled over his shoulder as Leonard nodded approval: they flashed by, doubled back and clattered past the guard. As if each huge, gray part of him had been primed and energized, he came to life. Ponderously, but with suddenly frightening power. He rose and lumbered for the door; with utter recklessness, for they still could have outraced him, the chief braked, darted back and headed for the stairs, followed by the furious Minuit.

"Filthy little bastards," yelled the guard, forgetting the door. Turning like a giant statue, he uncranked and pounded down the aisle after them.

Leonard froze, his laughter transformed to panic. "Hey *no-o-o,"* he shouted. "Hey *stop.* You've got it all wrong. They're just *playing."* The guard thundered past, ignored him completely and yelled, "Little bastards I break your neck." He reached the stairs and with surprising ease took them two at a time.

Leonard erupted. He sprinted past Sylvia and went after the guard knowing only that he must stop that power with a greater power. A wild, exciting power that had lain dormant all his life. The supercharge thrust him at that fat, official back, while somewhere behind him the tension of the museum was pierced by Sylvia's shrieking *"Leonard no."* Through his excitement he heard the hard clacketyclack and he realized she was somewhere behind him, imploring him to stop already, go home or to Radio City, *any*where but here. Sorry, his power said, but this must and *will* be done. Reaching for more bitterness, he drove himself after the guard. Up the stairs fled the tagline, Chief, Minuit, guard, Leonard, Sylvia. Into the Indian wars, past Geronimo and Sitting Bull, the prancing Custer, the businesslike Miles and Crook . . .

He felt the guard coming back to him. After two circuits the thick neck was ringed with purple, the strides hitting hard and flat. But *his* wellspring was still producing. He was aware, as he stocked up on indignation and disgust, that the clacking had stopped behind him and as he came back around the Apache he crossed in front of Sylvia, grinned and waved. Her face flashed past, white and gaspy and obviously amazed at how the intellect could blend with power. Then he was past her and driving for the guard who was beginning to waver slightly. The picture of bullying force collapsing before retribution could confront it sparked all his remaining strength, and gathering himself he launched into an arching, flying tackle. His timing was wrong and he hit the guard in the behind with his shoulder, but down he plummeted like a falling rock. Then they were rolling over and over. Leonard caught a glimpse of astonished (and suddenly aware?) face *"Jesuschristwadayoudoin."*

He shook his head and laughed wildly, marveling at how simple and painless an act of violence really was. The floor, the guard's strength simply did not exist. Swelling with inspiration, he pinned the guard in a long-forgotten hold, then sat on his stomach. "Just . . . be . . . quiet," he panted. "And listen . . . You must stop being a . . . bully." The guard glared and thrashed weakly. Leonard held him with ease while the heavy arms swung in syrupy slow motion. "Whoa, Nelly," he said, grinning. "Slow down, Poppa. Be nice now." The thrashing stopped. "That's better," Leonard said, "much better." The gluey body relaxed. "You going to behave now and stop picking on kids?" The guard glared at him with the specific know-nothing face that glared at field-trip classes. "Wellll?" The stupid eyes flickered and Leonard sensed the exultation of physical victory. "Well?" The eyes flickered again, at a spot behind him, over his head. For the first time Leonard became aware of the overpowering hush in the room. Only the guard's breathing intruded. And the suddenly smiling face beneath him. He jerked about. Just in time to see the two boys approaching Sylvia who was pressed against the wall. They stopped, poised. Then the white boy darted and like a cracking whip swept the purse from her hand. He flipped the purse in a delicate lead pass to the little Negro who was sprinting for the stairs. Then they were gone. Sylvia stared at her hands.

He felt a gentle heaving beneath him and looked down. The smiling face had regained its color and the lips were starting to work. Leonard wanted desperately to get off the man's chest, to run away from him and Sylvia and red men and white men. But he couldn't move. Nor could he blot out Sylvia's quiet sobbing, or her hands curled around the invisible pocketbook. Nor could he duck and escape from the words as they finally reached the guard's mouth and drove at him like an express train through the quivering, purple lips, asking the final, inevitable question, "Okay buster, you happy now?"

GARY
DIS-DONC

Your day is straight out of the textbook. *The* textbook.
Clock-radio. R & R. Swing out and jump down and shave
(every other day). Mix Wheaties. Crispy. Crunchy. Crispy
crunchy. Muss hair. Omit tie. Grab Falcon (convertible),
drag two, cut three, bank in. Squealing. Bruise tire against
curb. An inch from Mary Lou Konstanflaegel. That's correct. You couldn't make that up, could you? No. Mary Lou
Konstanflaegel. Hi Mary Lou. Hi. Do your paper, Mary
Lou? Yes. Dramatic. Top dialogue; Shakes-Mill-Will-
Racey-Bernie. Do your paper? Yes . . .

So all right, you pledgeallegianceamerica, you nod,
you agree, you go and snow. You chop up periods. Like so:
halves, quarters, octets. Shoot for less. It moves. Majors.
Minors. Throw out that basketball. Hi Mary Lou. Lunch.
You're halfway home. That's Mary Lou. Hi Gary.

You're Gary. You were meant to be Seymour or
Schloime. Or Milty. You're Gary. Gary Donk. Né Donk-
leberger. No snow. Honest. Listen, a liar you're not. So big
deal. Big big. The father of you, Nathan (Soc) Donk-
leberger made his killing in ladies' underwear, took out a
three-mortgage note, paid off in five months, bought a
Mercedes, a Falcon (yours) and a Volks. And you're Gary.
You have it made, Gary. All day, everyway, Maryann.
Y.O.U. Okay, you B-12'd, soft, pampered underachiever
you. You hit the eighth period and what happens. Everything. You kick the hipper-dipper and the hacking around.
You live. Oh Gary you live. Why? Listen well. *Écoutez, en-
fants:*

ELAN

That is a French word. *Élan.* Spirit. Dash. Drive. Flair. *Zetz.*
It is a way of life. Your way. All the way, everyday, Maryann.

It was Lou's and Joanie's and Boney's and Bouley's and
Vic's and Clem's and Ferdie's and Desperate Frenchy's.
Oh, you are dazzled, delighted, driven. You even have a
word for what you are. *Francophile.* Webster's unabridged.
A disease. It is. It is you. *Vous. Tu. Compris?* It is the reason
why. Your reason why. The reason why *vous tu* you are
transported, knocked out when up comes your number and
y-o-u are lifted out of paradise into paradise. *Un enfant du.
La chance* big. Main. The treetippy top. You. Gary Ben
Nathan Soc, you are tapped for "Students Across the Sea."
The big one. And it proves you could do it if you only tried.
You tried. For the first time. Oh how. And for achieving the
greatest improvement (no contest when you start below the
X line) you are rewarded. Yes. "This splendid young man,
who has worked so hard, who has earned his recognition
(oh he has)." Oh yes. Yes. The right reward for the wrong
reason. Yes, you will report back, you will inform, en-
lighten. You will do good. Yes . . . You will . . .

So. You're punctured, suited up, passported, visaed,
stamped, lied goodbye-to by suddenly materialized (and
bravely dry-eyed) parents, and on a lovely autumn-in-New-
York day, despite dreams of fluttering feathers, you board
Pan Am (for Daddy trusts only Yankee expertise). You discover learning by doing. Wild John Dewey. You suddenly
respect Lindy, politics and all, for flinging himself across
that ugly, green slash. Lucky Lindy. Unlucky? You get
stickyfeverish on long trips . . . *Mais oui,* you're building and
you know it, but you cannot stop. Willnot. What? Why?
Because.

Because nothing repeat nothing has ever lived up.
Ri-en du tout. General thumb rule. Nothing. Empire State,
Yosemite, Pike's Peak, Okefenokee, Kim Novak. Great put-
you-downs. You patsy you. So you fret, you recall. You tell

yourself. Well Paris is Paris, *c'est tout.* A city. Brick, water, peoples, history (ah), a city. Hedge against the big drop. The elevator. Pop. You outgun yourself this time. You know it. You know you know it. You know you know you . . . *Dis-donc.* Think. Thonk. Peripherally. With your slanty mind. How it must be . . . No, don't. Let it go. Leave it loose. Yes; but was Ernie right? Was he was he? And Gerty? And Jimmy J. and Emile and Guy and *Anatole.* Ah such a name. Maxie Tasmania. Gary Long Island. *Assez assez.* Francophile. File Franco . . .

Eat your package lunch and supper, lose time in great gobs and study some advanced algebra (for the first and last time) for relief. For headache take aspirin, for Francophiling take binomials. Hah? No. Heh. *Hein.* Ahhh. Finally you doze off and dream of fluttery feathers. Chicken you. Softly, smoothly into the green slash. Ugh . . .

At dawn you swim awake. You're still hanging up there. Under the pure white streaks of daylight. You feel . . . you don't know what. You look overboard and . . . *le voilà.* There. There, poking a naughty finger at you, dappling its roofs, stroking its grand boulevards, shaping, tubing its green. Its white. Oh. *Là.* Oh *là là.* The first time you saw Paris; Paris in the fall, it's grand it's true. You *vous tu compris* . . .

Alors, you have studied Michelin, traced, retraced Metro lines, dug into *contes drôles,* breezed with Athos, Porthos, Aramis, hit the Dart, played a little Quasi, developed a true Paree of the mind-set which must supersede the four-star, pumped-up Technicolored unreality. You think. This, you know, is necessary, this must be. It is RIGHT. Ahhh you are wrong. *Tout à fait.* As wrong as you hoped you'd be. *Trompé.* Trumped. It is there. Split through its

shiny heart, drawn, quartered. Waiting. Lafayette you are
here . . .

Le Bourget. Lucky Lindy. Lucky Gary. But no crowds,
no cheers. Yet. You feel the communion, sense it in your
Francophiling bones. You taxi to a soft stop, unbuckle,
hustle past Chambersburg, Pa., thank her and touch down.
Truly, existentially. You walk confidently through customs,
declare all and nothing at all. You ask, no demand, *où est le
bureau de renseignements? Renseigne-ments.* You stroke that,
glove it, hit it again. The agent does not flicker or give you
the American look. He points. *Merci.* Mercy. You bless Advanced Placement and audiolinguals, and you walk to the
bureau de. But of course. There. Right there, as confirmed,
reconfirmed, firmed, stands Jean-Pierre.

Jean-Pierre is French, oh is he ever French. Black turtleneck sweater, bell-bottoms, too much hair, shoes creaky-
stiff, great gloppy heels. French. You receive the solid
handshake, the solemn greeting. He collects baggage, fluffs
a redcap with a snapping hand and walks you out, piles you
into a Peugeot and steams you down through the guts of
your city. Along Haussmann and Woody Wilson, past the
grand *magasins,* the great magazines; you twist and quiver
and gooseneck and register. *Place de l'Opéra* and Coca Cola.
Buvez le. Madeleine and one hundred thousand shirts. Hey,
all you crazy, blasé *gens,* look around, see what you got.
Okay okay, time. Deeper still you arrow, to the far right, far
far. No touristy Bohème, no Georges sank, no *Champs,* but
all champs, down to where they clobbered poor, fat Louie,
where wild Oscar finally put down roots. To the street. *The*
street, printed in your headmap through all the negotia-
tions. *Écoutes: Rue du Chemin Vert.* Roll it around, caress it.
Street of the Green Way. Greeny Street. *Hein?* R . . . d

. . . C . . . V . . . *Vingt et un. Troisième étage.* Cognate *that.* Ah your stage. Your third. No your second, the French they are a funny . . . Oh it is small up there, on the *troisième,* dark, 150 years old, with *Figaro* johnny paper. It is three squares from République, two from Bastille, five from Lâchaise and it is *chez vous.* For a year.

And Madame Boncoeur she is Mama—tough, shrewd, miserly Mama. And Papa is Papa: little, moustached, world-warred, *vin ordinaired.* These people they are not absent. They are present. *Toujours.* Through the long drives. Through the Lux on Saturdays and the *bois* on Sundays. In the evening. Always *là.* From the first *enchanté* you know it. Home. *Chez vous.* Jeez you. How did you get born three thousand miles west. *Quel fromage!*

Alors. Mama, Papa, the maid and you. Wiseguy. Mama, Papa, Jean-Pierre and you. *Assez.* They are more than. They teach you. Larn you. Sure you've already lived with it for eleven years. Sure you're studying in the lycée Victor Hugo. History. *Histoires.* Get it? Got it. Gone.

Mais ici. Here with Mama, Papa, J-P and Greenway Street. LIFE stories. *Écoutes.* Mama is history no? Yes. Petty *bourgeoise? Non.* History. Live. Mama tells you herself. In the long, exquisite evenings, over *les bons repas.* After them. She tells. About her Mama and Papa. Ooohah they are a proud, these mamas and papas. Tough, *toujours* present. In Alsace, in Strasbourg. Along with the (ugh) Boches. Yes. They are (ugh) history too. *Hélas.*

Ripping through the quiet and the sunshine and the mamas and papas. Wilhelm and (ugh ugh) Bismarck. And strutty little Louis, long gone. Leaving mamas and papas and silent years of remorse. And the nation planning. *Pour revanche.* With *petites mamans* saying prayers for *liberté.* Until the day the lamps went out. No, went on. The redemption and the glory.

Papa screeching out in his taxi to meet the (ugh) hun and throw him back and you slog with him through the *moutarde* and the 75s. Beneath the dogfights (drunk many times with Nungesser, many times). *Écoutes,* Gary, those mutinies. *Boche* propaganda. *Menteurs!* After all, Gary, who won? Check. Who indeed. You could look it up.

Mama and Papa in *French* Alsace. *Avec le petit Jean-Pierre.*

Enter *le grand Jean-Pierre.* His face shining, clouding, shining, despairing. You gulp some red. You are swimming in glory and despair. You lean in. Mama and Papa strain, too. Strain back to the days of betrayal, of blackness, of rot, of avarice. You see it coming, you know it is coming, you are hypnotized. The six weeks. The six black feathers. They hit and you can hardly stand it. You are throwing away gasmasks, canteens, helmets. You run. The Imperial Guard wouldn't believe. They wouldn't. UGH.

You stagger off to bed and you dream of the rot and the avarice, the sell-out. The *poilus.* Running. Oh *assez.* Too *assez.* If you didn't know the ending you couldn't bear it. Ah but it is better this way. And worse.

So. Continue Jean-Pierre. And friend Claude, belted, raincoated, bereted. Enter the Maquis. OhGod the Maquis. Run with them. Through the wood. Bail out. Hit Dieppe. Set up the radio. Tear down. Set up. Claude, Jean-Pierre. *Le Lapin Agile.* They drive and hide through the sullied years, *marchés noirs,* deportations. How Mama cries and Papa's *moustache* trembles. Yes, Gary, yes, you can see it still. All about you. Look. *"Ici mort pour la patrie,* Marc Piedmond." *"Ici mort . . . pour la patrie . . ."* See, the bullet hole. Oh you see. You scoop it out. You feel it burn. A true friend, Marc, a fine boy, quiet, studious, like you, Gary. Gulp. But fed up to here. *Here.* Choked with it. Resisting it. Killed with it. You are crying now. So? They are too. Look, Nathan Soc. Gary is crying. This one. This bowl of ice. This lousy kid who got it so good he don't appreciate. See, Nathan, the tears. God forbid you should see. Yes, one is grateful. One appreciates. One cries.

What else does one do? How can one describe? Try. Well one drinks a *crème* with classmates at the Magots and watches American tourists. One studies ankles and *poitrines* and other important subjects. Like *les Anglaises* and *les Suédoises.* One raises a scraggly little beard and one goes in the evening with Marie and Gérard to the Flore and the Colombier and the Tabu. One digs *le hot.* One ignores the Folies and Pigalle and the Tower. *Au contraire.* One partakes, one absorbs, one becomes. Yes becomes. You. You transform. No. You become you. As the year jets by. Through the glistening autumn. Along the boulevards. Through Passy and Montparnasse. Through the bitter winter with no *chauffage central* and who needs it. From the Lux to Pick-the-Puss to Nelly on the burnt-coal toonerville. *Troisième classe. Toujours.* You are you. You genuflect before Napoleon, stiffen beneath the Arc, gorge on Austerlitz, Jena, Vilma. Once more you rip apart the Bastille.

Jean-Pierre whispering softly beside you, describing each thundering moment. A soundtrack. Narrating the *commune.* Pointing to the barricades. And Mama and Papa listening with pride over the wine and coffee as you burst out with your knowledge. Nodding. Approving. And remember, Gary, it is not all war and flame. It is beauty, too. Ohyes you know. Haven't you tiptoed through Versailles, shared with Louis, gazed with the Tiger into the mirrors, strolled the Bois, pondered with Rodin? All the beauty and the splendor. And glory. Jean-Pierre tells you.

Ah a fine one, Jean-Pierre. Always present. He never seems to work. Why should he? Since the Maquis it is all downhill. But do they bug him? Do they worry he should be something? Do they, Nathan? He IS. Nothing, repeat nothing is good enough for a Maquis, Nat. See? *Rien.* Neither wheels nor deals. It is obvious to Mama and Papa. It is obvious to Gary Dis-Donc. The true you. Jean-Pierre has performed the christening.

So, Gar Dee Dee, you ride with him. You fly. You scratch Bismarck and Laval. You listen to his recording of *Le Grand Charles* in London. You swallow, you cry, you fling your arms about Mama. You iceberg you. She hugs you. Understands.

Oh it is living inside out. Exposed. Sandpapered. It is (almost) too much. All the beauty and the glory. Wait. What? Not all glory. Jean-Pierre's face dims. He sighs. Not all glory, Gary Dis-Donc. There are still bad things, sad things. Betrayals. Who? What? Why? Where? When? Ah yes, *petit* Gary, there is. There is Indo-Chine. (A moment for Tassigny.) Mama and Papa are murmuring. There is Tunisie. Murmurs. There is Algérie. *Mon dieu* it is quiet. You've heard quiet but this is some quiet. You kiss, are kissed, blessed, and you say goodnight and slide into your soft bed and listen to the pahm-poom of the police and the Marne taxis and the quiet rustle of a thousand glorious years. You don't sleep.

Next morning, hard, cold, white, you are closer to your suffering, tragic, heroic family. You trudge off to school. You are thoughtful all through the day. Pensive, unresponsive. A quiet *crème* with Marie and Gérard. A set of doodles through Sartre. You have too much nothingness. You are full of nothingness. You close books and sigh. You walk home through the glory of République to the street of the Green Way. It is an evening for tragedy and heroism. Easy.

You meet Jean-Pierre. He is leaning against his scooter.

"Hello *ami*," he says. He wears the tan, belted raincoat and the dangling Gauloise.

"*Bonsoir,* Jean-Pierre," you say and you swing a little. "*Qué tal?*"

He gives you the wink and takes your arm. "*J'ai soif,*" he says. "Come on, a little red."

You nod, wink back. If a Shadyside status seeker says how about a beer, Gary, you wander away. J-P says Gary, dive through that window, come up saluting and whistling *Frou Frou.* And you're gone. You walk with him, swagger with him, wave at the good people of the *quartier,* the black sweaters, the horny-handed mamas, the flap-open skirts, the streaky hair. Your gang. Your *gens.* You check in at the Flambeau and stand up at the bar and grin and gulp a red in time with Jean-Pierre. Ahhhh, draw the rough sleeve across the mouth, hit the bar.

"*Encore,* Jacques." Jack is with you.

"*Alors,* Gary Dis-Donc," says Jean-Pierre, "and what did you study today?"

"Oh," you shrug, working a little accent into your English. "A little Sartre, not too much. Redon. And a rather nice lecture on the *entente cordiale* by the blind professor." You swig your red. "He's quite good," you say, "but he misses Clemenceau's essence."

"Ah," laughs Jean-Pierre. "You are a student, Gary. How I admire that. I was . . ." he shrugs, "a *coucou.* Always with the motorcycle. *ZZZZZT.*"

"No." You protest. "You've done your share. More. Hell you combine knowledge with action. This is all books." Do you knock down the *grand frère?* Hell you come up fierce.

"Oh," he laughs, patting the shoulder. "There have been a few moments. A few." He drinks. "A few, eh Jacques?"

Jacques grins and nods and pours two more reds. You drink and spin off just a little.

"Gary," Jean-Pierre says, "do me a favor, eh?"

Swim the channel? Take Verdun? "Yes, Jean-Pierre."

"Gary, here is a letter. Take it to the address on the envelope. Rue du Bac. By the river. You know? Okay?"

"Sure okay, Jean-Pierre."

"You're a good boy. You take my bike, eh . . . ?"

You're gone while he's still asking. You mount that scooter, gun that scooter down the Greenway and across history. *ZZZZZT* over the Pont Neuf. You juice it as you storm past the going-home office girls and the tourists, you swing it into Bac and dismount with Jean-Pierre's wild west swoop. You dash through the courtyard of number ten, punch the button and ride the *ascenseur* to the *sixième,* to Lamandre, A. You knock, wait, diddle. The door cracks, swings. You're asked in. You deliver your precious cargo and the two belted raincoats fuss over you and insist on a *café.* Well just one. You chat. You do very good.

"*Monsieur* Donc," says the tall raincoat, "you are not at all *américain.*"

You swell up. "*Merci.* The name is Gary. Gary Dis-Donc. That's what Jean-Pierre says." They roar. You balloon.

"Not at all *américain,*" says the shorter. "You are *sympathique.*"

You like that. You appreciate. You have another *filtre*. Then you check the time and nod. They nod. Respectfully. Shake hands. Respectfully. Wish you *bonne chance*, which you already have. You depart. Mount and fly away home. All in a half hour. You are purring. You are *sympathique*. The family Boncoeur is waiting dinner for you and mama scolds and you hug and kiss. *Sympathique*. You wink at Jean-Pierre, he clicks back. You sit down with your family. You eat, you tell about *your* day.

After dinner Jean-Pierre talks about secret transmitters in the Raspail station in forty-four. Then he swings into the main event. Liberation. It is an endless bedtime story. You never get enough. You go wild in the parade down the Champs. You clean out the rooftops, embrace the girls. You're hard, fierce, triumphant. You're you. No crying that night.

The next day you are in political science, around Kellogg-Briand, near the naval ratios, when you hear a boom-boom. Near the Concorde. The class looks up. Ohoh one of those infernals. A *plastique*. The blind one blinks the sightless eyes, pauses, then continues. The class bends forward and scribbles; he is tough, the *aveugle*. Well, a little danger is exciting, no? Yes. The class is quiet and nervous all day. Afterward you walk home slowly.

Jean-Pierre is leaning and smiling and holding another letter. Would you run over to Saint-Louis? Eh, Gary? Knock three times, then a fourth. Like so. Shivers. Big guys. You reach and take that letter, run to the curb, hop it and hustle crosstown. This time there are four raincoats. You're pummeled, congratulated, wined, and off you go. *Sympathique* you. Back home Jean-Pierre is pleased. Papa is deep in *Figaro* and the TSF blares. About four gendarmes who were blasted. Claude is here for dinner and he turns his nose up at the gendarmes. J-P smiles.

But you. You have begun to feel . . . something. You don't like to hear of wounded police, or wounded anybody. *Flics,* shudders Claude, turning up the nose. You don't quite understand. Don't quite . . . Jean-Pierre understands. He is patient.

"One must fight back, Gary. As in forty-two. One must not give in."

"But . . ."

"Betrayal. In the air. *Partout.*"

"But de Gaulle . . ."

His fingers crack. The room grows silent.

"Ah Gary, badly advised. Badly. And he grows old. Pétain was great once, but he grew old."

You listen to Jean-Pierre and everything comes clear. Everything.

"Remember," Jean-Pierre says, "Dienbienphu."

Oh you remember. As you stand and sing the *Marseillaise* with them, you remember.

During the night a whomp rattles your window and you snap up. In the dark your underachieving mind works. A lousy kid you are. A hacker you are. An ingrate you are. A dummkopf you're not. You are figuring. Whomps and scooters and raincoats. *ZZZT Ka-chung.*

And then a shadow leans against the door and blows a smoke ring. A patient shadow. The shadow knows. You wait for the answers. You get them. Slowly, thoughtfully. The answer to grandeur and historic mission and honor. Right here, Gary Dee Dee. On this spot. Very. Where Louis the Fat slept. Where Colbert connived. And Marat and

Charlotte made it near the end. And Ney and Coubertin clattered by on the way to Moscow. *Avec le grand petit.* Wow, you're up now and pacing excitedly as he digs in. He points out the window to République, to the barricades. Below, where Bismarck himself defiled the cobblestones. He spits on the floor. Bismarck, our friend now. *Ally.* You spit. You are with it now. You pick up and take it from there. You tell him about the betrayal and corruption, of the filthy Esterhazy and the moral rot. You accuse. You pace faster. You swear the blood oath of Saint-Cyr, of Sidi Bel Abbes; steal into the Alsace hills to gaze on the stolen provinces. The *élan.* It is pumping now. You won it and they lost it. The betrayers. Down there, Jean-Pierre? He nods. They goose-stepped right there? Yes, right there. *Dieu.* And here, Gary, in this very room, there once was a brother and a sister . . . You stop and fling your bitterness onto the bed. He talks. You see, Gary, it could have been done. In Indo. But for the sell-out on the edge of victory. Tassigny told us. He knew. Duplicity. Cowardice. You sit up. The hell with the wounded *flics.* They're with you or against you. You shake his hand. And then the raincoats enter. There, above all the duplicity and betrayal, above the grandeur and the sacred honor, you swear . . .

Oh you are busy busy. Swollen with responsibility. You delve into your essence. Plumb your range. Cleek the man of forty faces. Leaner. Against buildings. Molder. Of putty (not silly). Mixer. (A little nitro goes a fur way.) Compositor. Notes from your underground. Nuts. In a Clignancourt basement, from a hot mimeo. Silent, avenging angel in the night. Swift, resourceful. White hot. Hot. You. Gary Donc. Dee Dee. You have found you. You tinker, investigate, troubleshoot. Yes you. You perceive the soft spots, you suggest, point out, illuminate. You utilize (at last) that superb, nonsensical Shadyside education. You analyze, triangulate, equate; add here, take away there, make do. All this. You. Gary Dis-Donc. *Dis-Donc.* Serious, pale, intense, sideburned by day. *You* by night. Oh word gets around. About this you. *Figaro* mentions the elusive one. You paste that in the scrapbook.

And one night (naturally) you wind through the sewers, beneath Huchette, and there, with three Stens on the door, you shake hands with the grand gray shadow. The voice is solemn with respect. Gratitude. For Y-O-U. Ah young man, you are daring. Yeah. Clever. Yeah. You are . . . Lieutenant Donc. YEAH. He shakes your daring, clever hand. *Bonne chance,* Lieutenant. You, tight with dedication. And *élan.* You salute and disappear into the shadows, and flit home through the shadows, avoiding the Javerts who are mapped in your head. Dumb *flics.* Oh what dedication.

You emerge and saunter to the Green. Kiss Mama and Papa, wink at Jean-Pierre. Then retire and think and plan. You plan well. Next afternoon traffic stops on Vaugirard and threads its way around the gaping hole. While you sip your *filtre* at the Magots. You're on your way. To the treetippy top.

You discover this town. Rediscover it. This Valjean, *marché-noir* town. Dark, black, *dangereuse.* Yours. You smooth it, twist it, con it. Dashing, clever, resourceful.

Somewhere (where?) there is another life. A life? Well the mail says so. Silly, plaintive, Long Island mail. You build a pyre to that life. *Finis. Fin.* You're too busy fulfilling. Meeting, dispatching raincoats. Passing notes on Alexandre III. Below the petty palace. Hit here, flit there. *Adieu,* Nathan, Nathan's wife. Forget Gary. It is better that way. Infinitely. You'll see. (But read the papers.)

Alors, marchons. You slide on the high, thin blade. Each day higher, thinner, sharper. One day the highest. Sharpest. Jean-Pierre zings into Jacques' and interrupts your Pernod. Tells you (breathlessly) to pack. Wow! Shoot back, empty the drawers, snap the bags and run for Saint-Lazare. You make it. Of course. Just. You ride all night. Whispers. Laughter. Jokes. All for one. One appreciates.

You debark in Bruxelles. Where else? You whirlwind through the city, dash from house to house, double back. You teaser, you taunter. Desperate, daring you. Even as you hear the door smash, the footsteps clang. Louder. In that last, damp, desperate, beautiful basement . . .

Ah, the Bastille. You are calm now. *Tout à fait.* Gently smiling. Shrugging. You want nothing. Only what is yours. That which you have earned. That. Which. To share with Jean-Pierre and Claude and Jacques. And the grand gray shadow. To ride with them to Monsieur Le Guillotine. You have earned. You deserve.

You face the betrayers, the doublecrossers. The black-robed one enters. He bids you rise. He mouths all the nonsense: mischief, foolishness, silly, young, spoiled American, a spanking you deserve.

You're up there now. Alone. You grip the rail. When the Esterhazy doublecrosser opens his mouth to lecture the foolish young American, it is your chance. Big, main. You're ready.

Listen Nat, listen lady. Listen Joan, Boney, Tiger, Nungesser. Wherever you are. Do not despair, Legionnaires. *Courage, Pied-Noirs.* Hear this:

Vive la France éternelle.
Vive la gloire.
Vive Gary Dis-Donc.

MELANIE AND THE PURPLE PEOPLE EATERS

"Horsebleep?"

Horowitz looked into the phone and was positive he could see the thin, frowning teacher. She was even nodding.

"That's what she said, Mr. Horowitz."

"Miss Garaminta, are you *sure?*"

"I'm positive, Mr. Horowitz . . . Mr. Horowitz, if I may, I think our Bunny Development Specialist should chat with her."

"Who?"

"Our Bunny—"

"Hold it. Just hold it." He turned away from the phone, took three clearing breaths, returned to the phone, smiled into it. "Not yet, okay? I'll get back to you, Miss Garaminta."

"Don't wait too long," Miss Garaminta suggested.

"I won't. Oh, I won't. I appreciate your concern, I really do."

"Thank you, Mr. Horowitz. Have a nice day."

Horowitz looks at his desk, the wall, the clock, the window. He deep-breathes again, wads the latest interoffice nonsense, loops it toward the wastebasket. It bounces hard off the wall, drops. "Two points," he says absently. He goes back to work.

He paced the bedroom. Counterclockwise. Marcia put up with it, then removed her sleep mask, sighed. "Walk the other way, will you please? You'll make us both dizzy."

He stopped. Looked. "Aren't you concerned? *I* am. I'm paying that school goddam good money. I'm not crazy about everything they do, but if the child's teacher calls me at work, it has to be about something."

Marcia said very politely, "Are you assigning blame because I didn't hover over the phone?"

"Why should anyone interfere with all your projects?" he asked. "Why should they do that?"

"Mel, let us not parry and thrust. I have a terrible day tomorrow."

"All right." He balanced firmly. " 'Horsebleep' is not 'See Jane run.' "

"Agreed."

"Thank you." He took a step, balanced again. "Marcia, that is all she said."

"When?"

"Today."

"Wait. What did she say *before* 'horsebleep'?"

He looked down at her, shook his head. "Not a thing. Zero. She was quiet all day, until after recess. That's when she said it." He sat down suddenly. He was sweating.

"What triggered it?"

"How the hell do I know?"

"You didn't ask?"

He got up, began to pace again, stopped again, turned. "Jesus, I was too surprised . . ."

"Oh, for crying out loud." She rolled over in a neat ball, uncurled, thrust hard into the furry slippers.

"Where are you going?" he said.

"Next door."

"Wait. Don't get her up. Wait—"

The door was swinging even as he said it. He stared. The door swung again and Marcia stepped neatly back, Melanie draped on her shoulder. With easy strength she set her down in Mommy's Chair. Shook her gently. Melanie's eyes blinked wide.

"Honey," Marcia said, sitting on the bed, "did you use a sassafras word in school today?"

Melanie blinked. "I don't know."

"Reconstruct. Go back in your mind. Think about your day."

Melanie reconstructed. "I don't know."

"Honey, did you say 'horsebleep'?"

She reconstructed some more. "I think I said that."

Horowitz asked quietly, "What did Miss Garaminta do to make you say it?"

"Mel?" Marcia smiled up at him. "I don't think we should assign g-u-i-l-t."

He shrugged off the spelling lesson and said, "Please let me handle this. . . . What did she do, Melanie?"

"I don't know, Daddy."

"She must have done or said *some*thing."

"Mel, too much p-r-e-s-s-u-r-e."

"*What*, Melanie?"

Melanie's chin trembled. Marcia folded into the lotus position on the bed. "What he means, Melanie, is this: Could you possibly figure out why you used a sassafras?"

". . . I don't know, Mommy."

Bleep, Horowitz thought.

"All right," Marcia said, "we are not driving you to the wall; everything is under control. We are not excited and neither are you. If you don't agree, just tell me."

"I feel all right, Mommy."

"Fine. Pat pat, hug hug. Now, let's all put it out of our heads and go to sleep. Let it all float away. Go inside with Daddy, Melanie."

"All right, Mommy."

Horowitz opened his mouth, but Marcia shook him off. She sank back, adjusted her sleep mask. He hesitated, then gathered up the wide-awake Melanie and walked back into the yellow and blue bedroom. He walked her up and down for five minutes, felt her grow heavy and quiet. Then he eased her down under the electric blanket. He kissed her forehead, tucked her in, straightened up.

She opened her eyes, smiled up at him, and said, "Daddy, is Ed Kranepool over the hill?"

In the kitchen, after the peanut butter sandwich, he clasps both hands as if he is praying in *shul*. Then he lowers the hands in precise steps. Looks over his left shoulder, then back. Then wheels and whips toward first base. The runner is caught leaning; he's out by four feet . . .

"Mr. Horowitz," Miss Garaminta said with quiet gravity, "I assure you that is what she said."

"Please repeat it," Horowitz said. "I have paper and pencil."

Her voice was very professional. "She said, quote, It's like kissing your sister, unquote."

". . . Is that *all* she said?"

"Yes. That one phrase, all day. Mr. Horowitz, the context was somewhat bizarre."

"What . . . was . . . the . . . context?"

"Well," said the professionally concerned voice, "I had just asked her to pick up the visible boy in one hand and the visible girl in the other . . ."

"Yes?"

"And, well, she said it."

"She didn't say 'horsebleep'?"

"Oh, no, that was last Tuesday. She really hasn't communicated since then. Verbally. Until this. Mr. Horowitz, may I ask . . . would it have any . . . familial context?"

Speak English, he screamed silently at the wall. "I don't think so," he said calmly.

"There *is* a male sibling."

"She has a brother. Dan. He's a year and a half."

"That's a darling age. I hate to sound even remotely alarmist, Mr. Horowitz . . ."

What bleep. "Yes, go ahead?"

"I was just wondering if there might be a hint of confused sexuality. . . . Mr. Horowitz?"

"No way."

"I was just wondering."

"NO WAY."

"I have to be candid with you about my perceptions."

He stopped twisting his ankle. "I appreciate that, Miss Garaminta, I really do. But it's laughable. She was flirting with her grandfather when she was eight days old. No way, Miss Garaminta."

"Well, as I said, I do have to live with my conscience."

"Absolutely. I live with my conscience eight hours a day on *my* job. It isn't easy."

"Thank you, Mr. Horowitz."

"I'll be in touch, Miss Garaminta."

He swings from the heels. The ball screams in agony as it flies over the left-field wall. He walks out of the washroom feeling stronger if not better.

The next day they had a three-way conference—Horowitz, Marcia, Miss Garaminta. Horowitz listened, nodded, made good eye contact. Especially when Miss Garaminta said,

"It's a bit hard to believe that she verbalizes a good deal at home."

"Believe me," Horowitz nodded, "she has a splendid vocabulary for her age. Sometimes we can't shut her up."

"Not that we're in the habit of trying," Marcia murmured.

"Well," Miss Garaminta said, "I simply have to tell you that she's very limited here. And then there's her choice of subject . . . horses . . ."

"Kids." Horowitz smiled, shrugged. "I was hung up on Hotpoint refrigerators. I thought that was crazy. Ice cubes. Hotpoint . . ."

"I don't see the analogy," Marcia said.

Miss Garaminta said quickly: "It's merely that the horse thing is rather odd in a developmental sense."

"Really?" Marcia said.

"How's that?" Horowitz said, leaning in a little.

"Well, it's generally girls who are pubeing who are into horses. This is unusually early."

"She walked very young," Marcia murmured.

"Great coordination," said Horowitz.

Miss Garaminta acknowledged with a shrug, then said, "I'm sure that's all true. I simply raise the possibility that it's more than one of those things . . ."

The room was pregnantly quiet.

Miss Garaminta finally said, "Perhaps she *should* see our Bunny man."

"I hate to be so negative," Horowitz said, "but suppose we give her a chance." He smiled. "Maybe next week it'll be the stock market."

Marcia said, "What's your point?"

"My point is, this week, it's horses, next week it could be AT&T."

"If I may," Miss Garaminta said. "That could be overly simplistic."

"I agree," Marcia said briskly. "Let's give your man a try."

"Just an informal chat, Mr. Horowitz."

Horowitz looked at her and she nodded encouragement. He looked at Marcia.

"Why don't we ask Melanie?" Marcia said.

He thought that over. Miss Garaminta watched him.

"All right. Fair enough. But *I'll* ask her."

"Go right ahead," said Marcia.

He got up and walked next door. Melanie was stroking the Shmoo in the shiny Concorde jacket instead of punching him.

"Hi, poops."

"Hello, Daddy."

"Would you like to walk inside and answer a question?"

"Sure."

"Positive?"

"Uh huh."

"Okay, we walk."

He took her hand and they walked inside and he sat her down beside him. Everyone was quiet. Horowitz looked down at Melanie, who sat with her hands folded and her toes pointing in.

"Would you like to talk to a nice guy?" he said.

Melanie looked up at him.

"His name is Mr. Sitkin. He's the Bunny Development person."

Marcia said, "He could be very relaxing to talk to."

Miss Garaminta said, "He understands your age group."

Melanie continued to look at her father. He patted her shoulder and she nodded.

"Superstiff," she said with a shrug.

Milton Sitkin had three framed diplomas on his wall and wore a beige turtleneck.

"It's a rather unusual situation, Mr. Horowitz," he said.

Horowitz kept tightly quiet.

"I've had three conferences with her, including intake."

Horowitz remained quiet.

"I'll come right out with it . . . Here it is . . . I think we're dealing with some form of glossolalia."

Horowitz finally said, "Come on."

"I've consulted the literature," Sitkin said, "to confirm my initial impression. I think that's what it is."

Horowitz tried a tiny smile. "You mean religious double-talk?" He tried a tiny wink. "We don't even talk religion with her." He smiled and winked. "We're orthodox atheists."

"I see," Sitkin said without changing his face. "Nevertheless, I feel we're dealing with some form of tongues." He bent over a spiral-bound notebook. "I quote: 'A dollar bill is the glue.'" He raised his head.

"Are you sure that she said '*a* dollar bill'?" Horowitz said.

"In my notes I have the article."

". . . Could it have been plain 'dollar bill'?"

"It's possible. I use a bastardized Gregg. In any case, it's a pretty sophisticated statement for a five-year-old. Unless, as I suspect, we go back in time . . . Can we brainstorm this?"

"Sure."

"Was your family hit hard economically at some point? Say, the great Depression?"

"Well . . . my grandfather lost everything in 1930. But I never discussed *that* with Melanie."

"Then she knows nothing of that trauma?"

"How could she?"

"Of course. How could she?"

"Look, Mr. Sitkin, she's part of a group, right? Kids discuss money, right? With me it was dimes, with them it's dollar bills."

"Of course . . . Mr. Horowitz, how about this: 'You need the mow to get an oh.' "

"How do you spell 'mow'?"

"Why?"

"Well it could be . . . say, m-o."

"Or M-o-e. Is there a Moe in your family?"

"No."

"Moses?"

"NO."

"I see."

They waited. Then Sitkin said, "I'll tell you my professional position. Regardless of how fascinating the tongues thing may be, it rates nowhere in the taxonomy of cognitive functions."

"I'll tell you my position as a parent. I happen to think Melanie is a pretty bright kid."

"No argument." Sitkin smiled. "Mr. Horowitz, I'm just bending over backward to play it safe. I could get one helluva monograph out of this, but *she* is my top priority."

"That makes two of us."

"Then we're all together. Frankly, I think Dr. Bimway should have a talk with her."

"Who's he?"

"Our consulting psychologist."

"I thought *you* were."

"I'm the man in the trenches. We have to take it up-stairs."

Horowitz examined the diplomas. Returned to Sitkin. "I want to put that on hold for now. I'd like to discuss it with my wife."

"Of course. I wouldn't wait too long, though."

"We won't."

"Fine. To loosen up our chemistry a little, can I tell you what she said when I said good-bye?"

"Sure, you can tell me."

Sitkin returned to the notebook, flipped a page.

"That child said: 'It is not over till it's over.' " He peeled off his glasses and sat back. "Mr. Horowitz, that is positively Kierkegaardian."

"It is not EST horsemanure," Marcia said with her hands on her hips.

"I did not say 'horsemanure,' " Horowitz corrected mildly.

"Don't think for one moment I don't know what 'horsebleep' means," Marcia said.

"All right," he said. "I still don't want any EST horse-bleep. Sitkin was enough." He met her eyes.

"It is not EST. I have hold you a hundred times. Here's a hundred and one. It is a transpersonal approach to counseling."

"Fine. Perfect. Only let's deal with her in a more constructive way."

"And how will we do that? In front of the TV? This whole thing boils down to that, you know. Your cockamamie jockmanure, or bleep, or whatever you call it."

"I don't happen to buy that," he said calmly.

"No? Dollar Bill? Glue? Don't think I don't know. Your precious Bradley. Bill Precious Bradley."

"*Senator* Bradley."

"Don't get off the hook. Did his father's glue buy his Senate seat?"

"What the hell are you talking about?"

" 'Dollar Bill is the glue.' You told her that."

"His father was a banker. He didn't even go to Princeton on a scholarship."

"Who gives a bleep?"

"Lots of people. As for glue, it so happens Bradley was the glue that held the Knicks together."

Marcia sat down hard. "Christ."

"Well, he was."

"Christ."

"Stop saying that."

She looked him over. "Maybe," she said, "you'd prefer 'You need the mo to get an O.' "

"I'd *much* prefer that. It happens to be a pretty damn good rule of life: You need the momentum to get an ovation."

"Will you please stop? You are giving me a headache."

"I'd say you were giving it to yourself."

"God. Give me strength. Or some of those aspirins your Nolan Ryan eats."

"It so happens that Nolan Ryan does not *eat* aspirins. He *throws* them. Aspirin *tablets,* to be precise."

"God."

"And kindly leave Nolan Ryan out of it. He has his own

troubles; with all that magnificent smoke, he's barely above .500 lifetime."

She waited a good thirty seconds. "You should both eat it."

He waited, planned out the voice modulation, the spacing of the words. When he was completely ready, he said, "I thank you kindly. However, Melanie is still not going to your guru. Her karma remains intact. So does her mantra. And do not lay any EST guilt on me."

"*It is not EST.* You are so simplistic and negative I wouldn't believe it if I didn't hear it. But I did."

"Oh, you did."

"Mel, I'm getting tired. I want only one thing. I want that child to reacquire her energy awareness."

"Give her some sugar."

"Christ."

"Come on, Marcia," he said, trying a smile, "loosen up."

"I will loosen up," she said with total severity, "when the child gets the strength to surmount aspirin tablets, Dollar Bill, and the rest of your illicit world."

He leaped out of the lounger.

"Illicit? Illicit? I'll let you in on something, lady. My illicit world happens to be cathartic and therapeutic and maybe you just ought to try it."

"I'll take Ex-Lax, thank you," she said sweetly.

"So *I'm* simplistic and negative? Let us temporarily assume that, all right? But maybe, just *maybe*, this world you are rejecting out of hand is the one she prefers."

"She's five years old, *schmuck.*"

"So?"

"Teach her to dance on the head of a pin."

"That's an answer?"

"Yes. Here's another. I'm taking her to Terry Meldencarver."

"I cannot accept that."

"You'd better, sonny boy, because I am."

"The hell you are."

"The hell I'm not."

She took Melanie to Terry Meldencarver.

Meldencarver lived in an apartment with low ceilings and low furniture. He had on a beautiful toupee, which he could wear in the shower, and his nose was very short and thin.

"What do you think?" Marcia said as Melanie sat in the mandala room, drawing.

"I've seen it before, of course," he said in his quiet voice. "It's her oneness."

Marcia closed her eyes. "He's shattered her inner space, hasn't he?" She opened her eyes. He let the question sink in. Then he barely nodded.

"I'd have to agree," he said gently.

Marcia rocked a few times, caught herself, and said, just as gently, "I've had it, Terry."

"Easy, Marcia."

"All right, but I have. This is too much. I'm sorry, but it is."

He didn't say anything.

"What about her core, Terry?"

"I can't quite reach it."

Marcia focused on her quiet hands, then looked up, asked very firmly, "Can you do anything?"

"I'll certainly have to dissolve blame."

"Yes . . . Terry, do what . . . you have to do."

"Of course."

She examined her hands again, shook her head. "Have you noticed her body language?" she said.

"That's my business, dear."

"Oh, I'm sorry . . ."

"That's perfectly all right. Yes. She's very skewed."

"God. I know. Oh, I know. Terry . . . can you . . . restore her center?"

"I'll certainly give it my best shot."

Her hands jumped. "God, don't say that."

"Why not?"

"That's the way *she* talks now."

He reached over, touched her stiff fingers.

"Mustn't indulge in panic, Marcia."

"I know . . ."

"What else do you know?" he said, lifting her chin. She smiled and avoided the toupee and the nose.

"The universe always says yes," she answered with total repose.

Melvin:

We have a basic problem and we both know it, but I will spell it out because at times like this you lapse into your pseudo-stupidity. Here it is: I cannot and will not permit Melanie to be further trapped by your idiocy. Or to be paralyzed by it. Therefore she (and I) are going to work with Terry Meldencarver, and wipe that infuriating grin off your face. While we do, we will stay with my sister Adele. This includes Daniel. I am asking, telling you, not to interfere. Not now. She must get the chance, ultimately, to choose. For now, therefore, the child must give up your world or she is forever *consigned to wondering if Red Holman can win with five* schvartzas. *This I cannot permit.*

Sincerely,
Marcia Singer-Horowitz

He circles *Holman* and above it writes *SIC(K)*. Then he takes his evening walk. At the corner he jabs the lamppost with three violent lefts, smashes it with an overhand right. Refuses to yell.

He came home and ate a TV dinner. Then, while soaking his right hand in hot water and Epsom salts, he turned, with the left, to a cable sports channel and watched the Wolf-pack battle the Blue Devils in a dual swim meet. Then he switched to channel 10 for the Rangers and the Islanders, agreeing absolutely with all the Big Whistle had to say. During the breaks in the action, he flipped to channel 9 for the Knicks and the Nets, his head shaking at the condition of the Human Eraser's knees. During time-outs he clicked to WNYC for the CUNY tournament, where he yearned quietly for the Beavers, Nat, the NIT, the NCAA.

He maintained this routine for seven nights, coming home from work a bit earlier each afternoon so he could plunge into the action of the Boilermakers, the Wolverines, the Redmen, the Spurs, the Whalers, and the Flames, the Iceman and Magic. He also managed to pick up from the South the first optimistic stirrings of Tom Terrific and Louisiana Lightning.

On the eighth day he got up late, toughened his right hand with witch hazel, then called in sick. He ate a TV lunch, watched the Celtics and the Bullets on the Betamax, locked up, and drove across town to the Green Forest Lower School. He parked in a six-dollar garage and walked down the street to the school. He told the security guard and the lady at the desk it was a medical emergency.

"I hate to barge into your day like this, Miss Garaminta, but something's come up and I have to relieve you of your top problem child."

"You've come for Melanie," Miss Garaminta said.

"Oh, yes."

"Mr. Horowitz . . . I . . . well . . ."

"Is there a problem concerning my problem?" he said lightly.

"I'm afraid there is . . ."

"Well, we *all* have problems." He waited. Then: "I *am* her father, Miss Garaminta."

She touched her cheek, her hair, her cheek again; she'd make a good third-base coach, he thought, smiling with support.

"Oh, how I hate these family things," she said with a thin voice.

He felt a buzz, but said, "It comes with the territory. *What* family things, Miss Garaminta?"

She stopped with the hand signals.

He said, "You can be very candid with me."

"I know that . . . All right . . . Mrs. Horowitz gave me firm instructions not to allow anyone to pick up Melanie except Mrs. Horowitz."

"May I point out that marriage is a fifty-fifty proposition, Miss Garaminta?"

"Oh, I knew this would happen. I knew it. And I'd be caught in the middle. I told that to Dr. Meldencarver."

"Doctor?"

"Meldencarver. Melanie's therapist."

". . . Pepper-and-salt toupee? Bad nose job?"

"His hair *did* look too nice. The nose . . . was awfully thin . . ."

"Uh huh. *Doctor?*"

"That's what she called him . . ."

His hand ran through his hair. "Miss Garaminta, listen to me. A man who will change his looks will change his credentials. He's a doctor like I'm the Sultan of Swat."

"He . . . doesn't have his doctorate?" she said stiffly.

"Miss Garaminta, I don't even think he has a B.A. I'm not absolutely sure, but I know this: he is a *mister* and his major was hotel management."

She leaned against the receptionist's desk. He said quickly, "You've been candid; now I'll be candid."

". . . Yes?"

"My wife and I are having problems. Serious ones."

". . . I inferred that from . . . He studied hotel management?"

"And motel. Miss Garaminta, as a result of these problems, my wife has moved out and taken Melanie . . . Mister Meldencarver is squarely in the picture."

She stepped away from the desk.

"You *do* understand what I'm saying?" he said.

"I understand," she said quietly.

"I'm fighting a stacked deck, Miss Garaminta . . . She's probably told you things about me. She and the hotel man."

". . . *She* did. He just listened."

"What did she tell you?"

"That . . . you hit imaginary baseballs."

"What about voices?" he said evenly.

"No, oh, no, she never mentioned voices."

He leaned in. "Did your Mr. Sitkin tell you I was a nut?"

"Of course not."

"What do *you* think?"

"Why, it never occurred to me. A concerned parent . . ."

"Okay. Miss Garaminta, the woman who told you those things, who has really leveled some serious charges, is shacking up with a phony doctor. With phony hair and a phony nose."

Her eye contact faltered. The receptionist hunched over her *Time;* the security guard studied his keys.

Horowitz said carefully, "Melanie is smack in the middle. Between those two and her father."

". . . That man called himself 'Doctor' . . ." Her eyes tightened. She firmed up her thin chest.

"I have always been so ridiculously naive," she said. "Mr. Horowitz, I'll get Melanie for you."

They purred south on the Jersey Turnpike. Horowitz, Melanie, the warm, cozy car. The dashboard lights glowing and out of the lights the rise and fall of a local high school basketball game. They listened without saying anything until they crossed into Pennsylvania and the game faded.

"You can turn it off if you want to," Horowitz said. She promptly turned it off.

"Where are we going, Daddy?" she said.

He nodded at his headlights picking out the road.

"Greensboro. North Carolina."

"Why, Daddy?"

"The ACC tournament."

She was quiet, then settled back.

"Big hoops, Daddy?"

"The biggest." He glanced down, then quickly back. "You haven't seen pressure till you see this tournament."

"More than Super Sunday?"

"As *much.*"

She looked up through the windshield.

"Will the Wolfpack be there?"

"Of course."

"Daddy?"

"Yes?"

"Who was the leader of the Wolfpack?"

"David Thompson, naturally."

She smiled at him and they glided through the quiet glow of a small town. When they were clear of it, she said, "Daddy?"

"Yes, hon?"

"If you have David Thompson on your side, what do you have to do?"

"Alley oop."

She wiggled against her seat belt.

"Daddy?"

"Yes, doll."

"Why do the Tigers drive you crazy?"

"The slowdown, doll."

"How do you beat a slowdown, Daddy?"

"With a swarming D, of course."

She nodded, scrunched back, stared through the windshield. They were quiet in the sweeping circle around Philadelphia. When they were moving through the lights again, into Delaware, she looked up at him.

"Daddy?"

"I'm right here."

"Daddy, how do you beat a zone?"

"Outside shooting, poops."

"The ultimate weapon, Daddy?"

"Skyhook."

"What do you do with four corners, Daddy?"

"Hold a lead."

"Says who, Daddy?"

"Says the Tarheels."

". . . Daddy?"

"I hear you."

"Who needs desire?"

"Anybody who wants to win, luv."

She was silent, looked gravely up through the windshield.

"Seat belt all right?" he said.

"Uh huh."

As Washington loomed, she said, "Daddy?"

"Pit stop?"

"Not yet . . . Daddy, where did Al McGuire have Cousy?"

"Heck, in his hip pocket."

She bounced once, settled back. She was very still, but outside of Richmond she stirred.

"Daddy? Run to daylight?"

He glanced down very briefly.

"Lombardi," he said.

"Purple People Eaters, Daddy?"

"The Vikings."

"Shotgun, Daddy?"

"Roger the Dodger."

"Rockne, Daddy?"

"Go, go, go, go, go."

"What else, Daddy?"

"Fight, fight, fight, fight, fight."

". . . Daddy?"

"Yes, babe?"

"What do you have to tell Mommy, no matter what?"

He looked down at her and smiled, then returned to the road. "Eat the darn ball."

"What else, Daddy?"

"Swallow the apple."

"What *else,* Daddy?"

He nodded, tightened his mouth. "It isn't over till it's over."

She sighed.

They crossed into North Carolina and she looked up at him. "Daddy?"

"What, cookie?"

She wriggled against her seat belt.

"Daddy, if Mommy yells and screams, what do you have to do?"

He hitched up his shoulders.

"Daddy, what?"

He rolled his neck.

"Daddy?"

He pushed down on the accelerator, just a whisper.

"What, Daddy?"

". . . Give her a T," he said grimly.

"Daddy?"

"Tell her to take five."

"Daddy?"

"Sit her down for . . . a quarter."

"Daddy!"

He looked down. She smiled up and nodded. *"What,* Daddy?"

"KICK . . . BUTT," he said.

She sighed and said, "I'm going to take a nap now, Daddy."

She pulled the blanket up to her shoulders and leaned against him. Soon her head dropped against his arm.

He hunkers down over the wheel. He pulls out of the flow, weaves ahead, spots a Ford. He slides in behind it and picks up the slipstream. He feels the gentle pull, knows he is in splendid position. He checks the dashboard. Everything is ready. With concentration, intensity, momentum, and perfect rhythm, they race toward the checkered flag of dawn.

BUNNY BERIGAN IN THE ELEPHANTS' GRAVEYARD

"Johnny Weissmuller is dead. The Olympic champion, who was featured in the role of Tarzan and played the jungle king in twelve movies, died today in Acapulco. The temperature is thirty-one and we're in for some more snow . . ."

Axelrod stared at the top of the partition to his cubicle where the incredible shocker had come from. Over the top, out of Lotte Zwillman's portable radio that was zeroed into WPAT all day. Axelrod kept staring through five minutes of Hugo Winterhalter. Then he looked at the clock on his desk: 10:03. He slammed his desk drawers shut, locked them and walked out of the office.

Downstairs, he stood at the curb on 34th Street. The east-west traffic rushed by. Crowds jostled past. Sidewalk peddlers. Three-card monte man. Not a word about Weissmuller.

Axelrod walked to the corner. There was a popcorn store on the corner that featured strawberry, raspberry and tutti-frutti popcorn in the window. A skinny black kid, whose legs sprouted out of his sternum, was examining the rainbow of popcorn. His head was swaying to a heavy, implacable beat that came out of a satchel of music in his left hand. Axelrod walked over to him. They both watched a growing layer of red popcorn for a while, then Axelrod said: "Well, Johnny Weissmuller is dead."

The kid swiveled his head while his shoulders picked up the beat. "Yeah?" he said. "That a fact?"

"Yes," Axelrod said. "In Mexico."

"Nice an warm down there."

"That's one way to look at it."

"Friend of yours?" the kid said, shoulders moving.

Axelrod gave him a look. "He was *Tarzan.*"

"Oh. Real tough, man."

Axelrod nodded. A blue layer of popcorn was forming

and they both watched it grow. "I wonder," Axelrod said, "how Mia Farrow is taking it?"

The kid considered. "Real bad, I bet."

"Yes, I agree."

"Well," the kid said, "take it easy, man, we all gotta go sometime. You know?"

"I know."

Head and shoulders moving, the kid walked into the store. Inside, he pointed to some blue popcorn.

Axelrod looked around. The crowd was bustling by and he felt a little dizzy. He spotted the Hotel New Yorker across the street and, carefully, waiting for the light, crossed over to it. Walking softly, he entered the lobby. As soon as he did, a shiny young man came over. "Can I help you, sir?" he said.

Axelrod turned slowly, for he was still feeling a little dizzy. "Weissmuller is gone," he said in a quiet voice.

The young man was silent for a moment. Then he said: "Did he leave suddenly, or were there indications?"

"How do you mean?"

"Well . . were you together for a long time?" The young man's face was grave.

"He's *dead.*"

"Ah. I see. Would you like to talk about it?"

"As a matter of fact, I would."

The young man led him to a large black leather sofa set against the wall. It was very close to where the Terrace Room was supposed to be. They both sat down. The young man smiled encouragingly.

"Maureen O'Sullivan," Axelrod said, "has to be very upset."

"One would think so." The young man stopped smiling. "Were they related?"

Axelrod blinked a few times. "She was Tarzan's *mate.*"

"Ah."

"In a certain sense," Axelrod explained, "Mia Farrow is Tarzan's daughter. That's because Maureen O'Sullivan is her mother."

The young man said Ah again, but he seemed to be thinking it through. Finally he said: "Isn't Mia Farrow involved with Woody Allen?"

"Yes. She *was* involved with Sinatra. Rather deeply involved."

"Ah."

"You could make out a case that would position Sinatra as Tarzan's son-in-law. It depends on how you look at it."

"I see."

Axelrod nodded. The dizziness was easing up. He looked around. Shiny young people were coming and going and doing everything very quietly. He glanced toward the space that should have been the Terrace Room. His stomach jounced. He could hear the thin, nasal voice wrapped around "I Can't Get Started." He could see the trumpet pointing at the ceiling, could hear the incredible last note. He sighed. "I caught Bunny Berigan over there," he said.

"Were you in law enforcement, sir?"

He was on the verge of staring, but the young man was so polite. "Also Sonny Dunham," he said.

"I see."

He looked toward the Terrace Room. He was aware that the young man was asking if he'd like to read some of their literature because it might help. He turned and said quietly but firmly: "I'm quite satisfied with my religion."

"Of course. We wouldn't dream of tampering."

"I really have no desire to be a Moonie."

The young man's smile was very tolerant. "We are not at all bothered by pejorative terminology," he said. "The Unification Church can handle it."

"Okay," Axelrod said. He contemplated the Terrace Room again. They were both silent. Then Axelrod said: "I caught Kay Kyser in there."

"Was she a problem?"

The young man was still nodding encouragement as Axelrod walked out.

He walked uptown to 43rd Street. Continued east to Seventh Avenue. Stopped. He stood at the curb. And studied the Paramount. Only you couldn't really call it the Paramount because it was so naked. The marquee had been sheared off and there was no lobby. There was this building but no marquee and no beautiful lobby. Or a lineup that plugged into the lobby and snaked around the block. Still he remained there, even though he was bumped by at least a dozen people as they hurried past. To see a skin flick or male burlesque. He finally hitched his shoulders and walked away to 42nd Street. Crossed and entered Herlihy's Bar. He ordered a beer on tap, drank it quickly and ordered another. Halfway through that one he turned to the man beside him, who was also drinking beer on tap. The man had bushy gray sideburns that dropped beneath his earlobes. His earlobes were fuzzed with gray hair.

"Weissmuller is dead," Axelrod said.

The man stopped his glass in midair. "Johnny Weissmuller?"

"Yes."

The man finished his beer and set it down. "Oh wow." He shook his head and his earlobes wobbled. He held up an empty glass. "Here's to Tarzan," he said solemnly.

Axelrod held up his glass. "To Tarzan. And the greatest Olympic champion in history." He finished his beer.

"I'm with *you*," the man said. Axelrod waved for two more beers. When they came he said: "To Jane." The man said, Check, and they drank to Jane. The man nodded at Axelrod. "Oh that Maureen O'Sullivan," he said.

"Yes," Axelrod said.

"In that sarong."

"It wasn't exactly a sarong. It was a two-piece outfit. A small, loose brassiere type of garment and a piece of cloth down below."

The man shrugged. "Same difference."

"Not really. A sarong—"

"Okay, forget it. It was some kind of outfit, wasn't it?"

"Oh yes."

"And could she wear it. Some Janes you would think they were wearing horsehair. Not her. She wore it like she was proud to be wearing it." The man considered. "And a little bashful."

"Yes . . ."

The man sighed and held up his glass. "No wonder Boy came along. Here's to Boy."

"To Boy."

They finished their beers. The man shook his head and his earlobes wobbled. "So he checked out?"

"Yes. In Acapulco."

"Funny place for Tarzan."

"I guess."

Axelrod ordered two more beers. The man sipped

thoughtfully, then turned. "Buster Crabbe went recently, didn't he?"

"That's right."

The earlobes were wobbling again. "All the guys with *cojones* and biceps. And look at us." He patted his gut. He looked at Axelrod. "I wonder if Lex Barker is still around?"

"No. He's gone too."

"You sure?"

"Positive."

"Wow. Every Tarzan. Gone with the wind."

"Not every. Just the ones that counted. And you can narrow that down to Weissmuller."

The man continued to sip his beer. "Sure he was great, no argument. But I'll tell you, I always liked Lex Barker."

"What in the world for?"

The man shrugged thick shoulders. "Who knows? You prefer something, who knows?" He smiled into the mirror behind the bar. "Maybe because he was married to Lana Turner."

Axelrod stared at the mirror. "So was Artie Shaw. Do you see him as Tarzan?"

The mirror-smile, again. "Hey, they can do a lot in Hollywood. Tarzan and his clarinet."

Axelrod didn't smile and the man turned. "Nobody respected Weissmuller more than me, but he wasn't *God.*"

"Neither was Lex Barker."

"I didn't say he was, okay? I merely said for my money he was right up there, okay? It happens to be my opinion and it's still a free country." The man turned back to the mirror and winked into it. "If you want a second opinion, ask Lana Turner."

Axelrod didn't ask Lana Turner. Or anyone else. But

he did poke the man on his wobbly earlobes. And was thrown out by Herlihy.

He walked quickly past the movie houses on 42nd Street and he was trembling. For he was remembering how he and Scott Lupowitz would fight over Weissmuller and Buster Crabbe. He was remembering how Lupowitz had plucked Crabbe out of the blue and made him his quintessential Tarzan. His exact words. And stuck to it even when he told Lupowitz Crabbe's first name was really Clarence. Made no goddarn difference. Not with Lupowitz, who could drive you crazy with things like that. Give you the shirt off his back but drive you crazy.

He headed for the subway.

For most of the ride he kept his eyes closed, but at the exact right moment he opened them. Yes. He got off and walked upstairs into the Bronx. It was a bone-cold day and it was even colder here because of the empty lots. There was a building here and there, but that didn't stop the wind. He leaned into the wind and began to walk. To Washington Avenue. And 172nd Street. And there he stopped. The corner was an empty, rubbled lot. Beside it was an apartment house with black holes for windows, plus a few decals that covered the black holes with paper windows. As if the apartment house was wearing pasties. He folded his arms against the wind.

"You lookin for somethin?"

A tall boy in a leather jacket and jeans by Sergio Valente had asked the question. He stood there, with his hands, except for the thumbs, thrust into his jacket pockets. An extremely short, thin boy, also in a leather jacket and jeans by Sergio Valente, stood beside him. Or rather, rocked beside him, for he couldn't keep still, except for his hands, which were also thrust into his jacket pockets. Except for the thumbs. A few feet from the boys was a terribly thin girl, also in a leather jacket, but with khaki pants. Her hands, including the thumbs, were shoved into the rear pockets of her pants.

Axelrod said, "In a way, yes, I'm looking for something. I should say someone. Scott Lupowitz. I doubt that I'll find him."

"You never know," the tall boy said.

"Thas right," the short boy added. "You never know."

"That's true," Axelrod said. "You don't."

"If we see him," the tall boy said, "we say you lookin for him."

"Oh yeah, we say that," the short boy said, rocking hard.

"Thank you," Axelrod said. "If you do see him, tell him Tarzan has gone west."

"Taza?" the short boy said.

The girl suddenly took her hands out of her pockets and pounded her chest, one fist at a time. The tall boy smiled, the short one threw himself to the sidewalk, rolled around, bellowed with laughter, bounced up, stopped laughing and resumed rocking.

The tall boy said: "Oh him."

"Yes, him," Axelrod said.

"Went to the West Bronx?"

"Just west."

"Sure, we see him, we tell him."

"Thank you."

"You welcome," the short boy said, rocking. "How bout a present for the club?"

"What club?"

The tall boy said quickly: "The Tarzan Club." He drew a hand out of a pocket. So did the short one. As he did, he took a jerky step toward Axelrod. Axelrod shifted his weight from his left foot to his right and the boy jumped back. The girl cackled.

"Who you laughin at?" the short boy demanded, now rocking sideways.

"Your mother," the girl said.

He glared and she cackled again.

The tall boy said Shoot, then Hold it, hold it, time out. He shook his head and looked very depressed. "How come you two always mess up?" he said with great sadness.

"Ax her," the short one said, pointing.

"Don't you point no finger at me," the girl said.

The boy dropped his finger and rocked in wide circles. The tall one clapped a hand to his shoulder and slowed him down. He said, nodding: "He got a point. When it come right down to it I kin never count on you."

"Tough," the girl said. Her eyes were slits.

"Leave her alone," Axelrod said.

The tall boy said very slowly: "What was zat?"

"Why don't you cats behave and go home?"

The short boy jumped, then rocked back and forth. "Who you talkin to, man?" he demanded.

The tall one braked him again and said: "He talkin to us cats. Hey Pop, better watch out or I git my granfather after you."

The short boy doubled over and gasped for breath. Between gasps he kept saying: "Oh man." When he straightened up the tall one's iron hand kept him still.

Axelrod said firmly: "Be my guest. Now please scram."

"What?"

"You heard him," the girl said. "Get lost."

The tall boy gazed at her, then cuffed the short one on the back of the head. "I don't believe it," he said with total amazement. "She like it ol an dried up."

"I don't believe it," the short boy said under the restraining hand.

The tall one gazed in wide-eyed surprise, then cuffed the short boy again and laughed softly. "Shoot," he said, "les split, I can't stand it. Hey Pop, okay if us cats split?"

"That's terrific," Axelrod said.

The tall boy said to the girl: "Go easy on that bad ol cat." He turned sharply and walked away with bouncy strides, his hands, except for the thumbs, jammed into his pockets. The short boy blurted out: "Yeah, go easy on the bad ol cat," and bounced after him, his hands, except for the thumbs, jammed into his pockets.

Axelrod turned to the girl and said: "Thank you, Miss."

She suddenly blushed. "Ah, they make a lotta noise, but they got no brains."

"Thank you anyway."

He looked down at her. The chest she had pounded was as straight as a ruler. She probably didn't hit 90 pounds. *"Como se llama, Usted?"* he said carefully.

"You talk pretty good," she said with a smile. "Juanita. How bout you?"

"Pop," he said.

"Ah," she said, "I tolyou they got no brains."

It came out and he hadn't even reached for it: "Bunny Berigan," he said.

"Thas a cool name."

He saw Bunny in the Terrace Room, blasting at the sky, bowing solemnly. "Yes," Axelrod said, "I've always liked my name."

She looked up at him and blushed again. "Can I buy you a Coke or something?" he said.

She studied him with her hands in her back pockets. "I don't hustle," she said quietly.

"I know that."

A smile replaced the severity and her face softened. "I oney drink Smirnoff vodka and Schweppes tonic."

"Fair enough. *Dónde?*"

"Be my guest," she said with the smile that transformed her face.

She walked him to Third Avenue, to the Dorado Club. They sat at a table and the bartender came over and took their order. Smirnoff and Schweppes for her, *cerveza* Bud for him. The bartender's name was Billy and he had a deep tan and wavy salt-and-pepper hair. She said, Billy, this a friend of mine, Bunny. They shook hands.

"Bunny know Tarzan," she said confidentially when Billy returned with their drinks.

"Knew," Axelrod said. "He died today."

"Johnny Weissmuller died?" Billy said.

"Yes. Today."

Juanita said: "He useta live up here."

"Johnny W. lived in the Bronx?"

". . . That's right," Axelrod said.

"Did he swim in Orchard Beach?"

"Sure."

Billy slapped his apron. "I love it. Didn't I tell you they *all* lived in the Bronx?"

"Yeah, you tolme," Juanita said.

"I love it." He patted Axelrod on the arm and walked back behind the bar, stopping to point at their table. Juanita sipped her drink delicately, set it down carefully.

She ignored the stares, said: "One thing I can't do, thas swim."

"You never had a teacher like Weissmuller."

"Ain't it the truth," she said with a sigh.

He drank his *cerveza*. "You know," he said, "I'd love to see where we used to hang out. But I'm sure it's gone."

"You never know. We ain't *all* bombed out."

"Of course not. That was gauche. . . . It was on Fulton Avenue. . . . The Castle . . ."

"That place? Thas still there."

"Are you sure?"

"Sure. Still there. Not one bomb."

He smiled gently. "Would you like to show it to me?"

"Okay. I oney drink one Smirnoff at a time."

They walked to Fulton Avenue and The Castle was there, all right. Except that, across the marquee, instead of TAR-ZAN AND HIS MATE or THE ROAD TO GLORY, it said, in huge white letters: CHURCH OF THE HOLY WORD, REVEAL, REPEAL, REPENT, RELENT. 8 P.M. THURS. SAT. SUN. REV. MICKEY.

"The place you useta hang out," Juanita said.

"Yes."

"See? Still there."

"Yes, it is . . ."

"Well," and she shrugged the blade-thin shoulders, "Mickey run the show now."

"I see."

"You wanna meet him?"

"You know him?"

"Sure. I know everybody." She took his hand. "Come on."

There were still a few clouds on the ceiling, and the mural was still on the wall. But Gable's teeth were black-ened and Loy wore a Vandyke. He could smell Lestoil. They walked down the center aisle, past the fifth row, where he would sit with Lupowitz and Lionel Klein. They climbed the steps at the side of the stage and walked back behind a white curtain. A man in a silver suit got up from a rolltop desk. "Well, well, Juanita in person," he said in a deep voice. *"Bienvenida.* And welcome to you, sir."

"Hello," Juanita said. "Reverend Mickey, this a friend of mine, Bunny Berigan. He useta live aroun here."

Reverend Mickey shook his hand firmly. He was very big, very neat, very black. "I would imagine you spent some time in this particular location, Mr. Berigan," he said.

"Yes, I did . . ." He kept himself from glancing back to the stage. Elspeth Brownleigh had been elected Queen of The Castle on that stage . . .

"Are you doing an article on the area?" Reverend Mickey said.

"An article? No . . . just visiting." Elspeth in a blue bathing suit. High heels. Turning shyly. Lupowitz whistling. Klein smiling . . .

"He was a friend of Tarzan," Juanita said. "He jus died."

"The noted Lord of the Jungle?" Reverend Mickey said.

"Yes . . . Johnny Weissmuller. He died today." Elspeth was a dead ringer for Tarzan's mate . . .

"Oh I *am* sorry. Would you like to pray for him?"

"I have."

"Of course. He was a great man in his day."

"Yes, he was."

"Alas, times change."

"Yes . . . they do . . ." There were stories about Elspeth . . . rotten stories . . .

"I know how it is, Mr. Berigan."

"I'm sure you do . . ." One rotten story, Lionel Klein and Elspeth, that story . . .

"Juanita, will I see you this weekend?"

"Sure. Jus tell the Holy Virgin."

"She would understand," Reverend Mickey said with a smile.

"Sure. She give me a look an report me to my mother."

Reverend Mickey continued to smile. It was getting warm back here. Axelrod reached for his wallet, peeled out a ten-dollar bill. Reverend Mickey raised a hand. His silver sleeve glittered under a fluorescent light. "I haven't done anything," he said.

"Take it anyway," Axelrod said.

"All right. Thank you. For Mr. Tarzan. Thank you." He slipped the bill into the top drawer of his desk. "Come again, Mr. Berigan. And bring Jane Porter with you."

Elspeth was smiling shyly over her Queen's bouquet and Lupowitz was whistling and Klein was looking as innocent as Boy as they walked out of the Church of the Holy Word . . .

"Jane Porter live up here too?" Juanita said. They were walking slowly along Washington Avenue.

"Yes. She and Weissmuller were very close."

She shook her head. "That Mickey. You name it, he done it. Or know it."

"So it seems . . ."

"Well, he had enough time to learn. He done five in Attica."

"Attica? Prison?"

"You know some other Attica?"

"Well no. But he's so . . . so . . ."

"Yeah, he is. He sure is. Mickey gonna own the Bronx some day."

"He seems so . . . straight . . ."

"He straight, all right. Now. He got the call in stir. Read a thousan books an got the call. Maybe Jane Porter work up there an help him get the call." She smiled her softening smile.

He smiled back. They came to the rubbled lot where they had met and he stopped smiling. Right there Axelrod had been 2B, Lupowitz 4D. He stared, then turned. "Juanita, it's been a real pleasure."

"Likewise. You goin home?"

"Well, downtown . . ."

She thrust her hands into her back pockets and shrugged.

He said: "I'm really going down to the Polo Grounds. Lupowitz and I spent a lot of time there."

"Yeah? I know someone live in the Polo Grounds. Tina Irizarry."

He looked down at the tough, severe face. "Would you like to come down with me?"

"Meet Tina?"

"Sure."

"Yeah, all right, but if you wanna be alone . . ."

"I'd like you to come," he said gravely.

"Okay." She smiled and her face came alive. "You like Tina, she crazy but smart, like you."

The Irizarry apartment was on the 12th floor. If you dropped a plumb line from the living room you would hit first base. Irizarry *padre* and *madre* were still at work and Tina was sitting three little brothers who were staring at a color TV with the audio turned down. Juanita had introduced him, explained that he had once lived in the Polo Grounds. He had glanced at the short right-field fence when she said that. Tina, who was very plump and had a mountain of coal-black hair, said she had cried every minute the time they went back to San Juan. Juanita remembered that very well. She patted his hand. He smiled and looked out the window. A big-league pop-up would just about reach the apartment . . . One of the kids squealed. Tina shushed him.

"Hey," Juanita said. "Bunny tol Tony an Mouse where to go."

"Oh great," Tina said happily.

"They almos died."

"Great." Tina's mountain of hair fell over her forehead and she shoved it back with both hands. "Thas the oney way with them idiots."

"The oney way," Juanita said, nodding.

He cut his eyes to the window; the throw was coming in from deep center field . . .

"Yeah," Juanita was saying, "Mickey try an convert me again."

"Not again?"

"Oh yeah, I'm tellin you. Ain't that right, Bunny?"

"What?"

"Dint Mickey try an lean on me?"

"Well, in a way, perhaps . . ."

"Hey, no perhaps. You don't know him. *I* know him."

"You tell him where to go?" Tina said.

"Sure. But in a nice way. Weren't it a nice way, Bunny?"

"Oh yes. You were very polite. Yes. She was very polite." The ball was hung on a clothesline over the shortstop's head; he leaped, missed it . . . Suddenly he stood up.

So did the girls, Tina pushing her hair back. *"Muchas gracias,"* he said.

"You welcome," Tina said.

"Hasta la banana."

They screeched with laughter. The boys stared, then returned to their TV. "Oh man," Tina said, "thas cute."

"Dint I tell you on the phone?" Juanita said.

"Oh yeah you did."

He looked out the window again, at the pitcher's mound. From a distance he could hear Juanita: "Don't he look like him?" Could hear Tina: "Oh yeah, you right." He turned back. "Look like who?"

They shrilled in unison: "Hal Linden!"

"Oh," he said.

Juanita said: "Do I ever lie, Tina?"

"No, you never lie. Bunny, that girl she never lie. Believe me. That girl she cut off her tongue before she lie—"

. . . The second baseman was gliding toward the bag. He nicked it exactly as he took the throw, leaped to avoid the gleaming spikes, spun, uncorked . . .

"Yes," he said. "That's it. That's my high school." He stared up at the building.

"No more it ain't," she said.

"No. No more. But I loved that school."

"Thomas Harris?"

"Townsend. Townsend Harris."

She looked the building over, shrugged the skinny shoulders. "I never love no school. I don't hate it but I don't love it." She shrugged again, pointed with her head. "My cousin Gerry he go to CCNY over there. Study day an night."

"So did I. Lupowitz and I."

She patted his hand. "You an Loopaloop."

He nodded and waved at a corner window on the third floor. "American Studies," he said. "Right there. We had a great teacher, Mr. Werkman. He was a pacifist, always lecturing us on the terrible root causes of the Great War."

"Gerry all over." She shook her head hard. "You open your mouth an he find a war. Don't *never* get him goin on Vetnam."

"Yes," he said. "We argued a lot, too."

"Over Vetnam?"

"No, but things like it . . ."

"I never seen *nobody* argue like Gerry. He take after his father. Oh man they put on a show."

"So did we," he said with a smile.

"You an your father?"

"Yes . . ."

"What you fight about? You don't hafta tell me."

"I'd like to tell you. About the trumpet and the violin."

"What about them?"

He gazed up at the window. "I played trumpet. I was quite good. Mr. Werkman, who was also the band man, said so . . ."

"Yeah, Bunny?"

"Yes. My father called him Paul Whiteman. He said this is none of your business, Mr. Whiteman. He went out and bought me a violin. A very good violin . . ."

"The hell with that, right?"

He looked down at her. "Right."

"You still play the trumpet?"

"No. Never. No."

"Gerry got a guitar an he don't play neither . . ."

He gazed at her. Her shoulders were hunched against the wind. "How old are you, Juanita?"

"Oldern you think. Twenty in a little while."

"How little?"

"Seven months."

"Yes," he said and she gave him the brightening smile, "that *is* older." Oh Lord, two-oh. He'd hit it outside Saint-Malo. Lupowitz never made it, missed by thirty-three days on Tarawa . . . Lord, two-oh . . .

"You had enough high school, Bunny?"

"What?"

"How bout goin someplace you an Tarzan went? The zoo?"

"No, we didn't go to the zoo." He looked down at her. "I met my first wife when she was your age, give or take a month."

"You wanna go where you met her?"

"*No.*"

"Okay."

He jerked a hand over his shoulder. "It was right over there."

"Yeah?"

"Lewisohn Stadium. It was a concert. A turkish bath of a night. Heifetz . . ."

She smiled her transforming smile. "Heifetz an Lupowitz." He didn't return the smile. "You sure you don't wanna walk over?" she said.

"Positive. It's gone anyway."

"How do you know?"

"I *know.*"

"Okay, Bunny."

He refocused on Townsend Harris. "I went to concerts with her; she'd never deign to go to the fights with me."

"That ain't fair."

"Tell that to *her*." He stared at the window and began to relax. "Oh well, we broke up," he said.

"Over the fights?"

"Plus a few other things." He looked down at her.

She hunched against the wind. "How many wifes you had, Bunny?"

"I'm working on my third."

She wrinkled her face and shrugged. "Lotsa luck."

He patted her hair; she made a mouth and pulled away. "Come on," he said, "I'll take you home."

"I know howta go."

"I'm sure you do. I want to. Okay?"

She thought it over very seriously. "Okay. This place ain't doin too much for you anyways."

She lived in a project on Webster Avenue. Across the street was another project called Butler Houses. He kept looking at it as they approached her entrance. Then it clicked: Claremont Court. She followed his eyes. "You live over there, too?" she said.

"No. But Lionel Klein did."

"Friend or enemy?"

He almost patted her hair. "A little of both."

"Uh huh. Like me an Teresa Santiago."

. . . Klein and Elspeth . . . Lupowitz giving him the lowdown . . . "What the h," he said. "On balance he wasn't so terrible . . ."

"Neither is Teresa. Jus be careful."

"Yes, be careful . . ." He turned away from Claremont Court.

"What happen to Klein? You don't hafta tell me."

"No, but I will. He was hurt in the war. At Salerno."

"That in Vetnam?"

"No." He glanced at Claremont Court, then suddenly held out his hand. "It's been a genuine pleasure, Juanita."

She reached up and gave his hand a quick shake. "Likewise."

"Maybe I'll see you again . . ."

She hunched her shoulders. "Maybe . . ."

"Is this your regular day off?"

She peered up at him. "For now. I'm lookin aroun. But it gotta be good. I had it with jerks incorporated."

He touched her shoulder and she didn't pull away. "Tell Tina I enjoyed meeting her."

"Sure. She call tonight. I know Tina. Talk for an hour."

"Tell her Hal Linden sends his regards."

"Are you serious? Thas all she gonna talk about. I actually seen that girl freak out over Hal Linden."

He walked quickly away without asking, Who's Hal Linden?

He didn't head for the subway, he headed for Tremont Avenue. And when he reached Tremont he kept going to Honeywell. And there it was and without any rubble, or black-hole windows, or pasties. But one problem, and a major one. Instead of AXELROD AND SON DRY CLEANERS, the sign said OTB. He looked through the window and let his grin blossom. A lady with white hair, who had a little of Mama, a little of Grandma, grinned back and held up three fingers; she'd hit the ninth race triple. He gave her thumbs up, then cleaned off the grin. Mama and Grandma had once gone in partners on the Irish sweeps; Papa found out and gave them both holy hell in front of everybody.

He walked away fast.

He didn't slow down until he reached Claremont Park-

way. Only then did he clutch into the old excitement and
head for Boston Road. As he walked he could feel on his
forearm Mr. Brownleigh's immaculate Palm Beach suit,
Mrs. Brownleigh's silk skirt, Elspeth's pongee blouse. He
stopped. The dark, cool, aloof house wasn't there. At least
he wasn't staring at Hiroshima. It was a firehouse, a new,
clean firehouse. He could hear Lupowitz, the fastest mouth
in the East: Hey Axel, put out the fire!

He walked.

It was a little after eight when Axelrod entered the Church
of the Holy Word. Reverend Mickey was standing just inside the door, shaking hands, chatting with everyone who
came in. He had changed from a single-breasted silver suit
into a double-breasted silver suit. He pumped Axelrod's
hand cheerfully and said: "Well, Mr. Berigan. I'm de*lighted*
you decided to join us so soon."

"I can't stay too long . . ." Axelrod said.

"As long as you wish. It's up to you."

". . . Where should I sit?"

"Anywhere at all. You choose. Make yourself comfortable all over. Please excuse me?"

"Of course . . . you go right ahead . . ."

Reverend Mickey turned to a mother and her two boys
and told them cheerfully it was so nice to finally see them
and better late than never. Axelrod walked slowly down the
center aisle and sat down one seat in. Lupo liked the aisle
because he went to the bathroom a lot, and Klein liked the
third seat; he had this thing about threes.

Suddenly the houselights went down. Axel closed his
eyes.

When he opened them he didn't see the lion growling,
or Lady Columbia. He saw Reverend Mickey. Huge and

silvery. Standing very still under a spotlight, behind a podium.

"Good evening," he said. "How are you all tonight?"

"*Ready,*" came the answer, like a college cheer.

"Excellent." Reverend Mickey spread his silver arms wide, then slowly dropped them. "Now then, the next question. What are we getting ready to *do?*"

"*Reveal,*" came the cheer.

"What do we do with that item?"

"*Repeal.*"

"And after we rid ourselves of prohibition, inhibition and exhibition, what's next?"

"*Repent.*"

"I hear you. Very loud, very clear. Now. You are strong. With that strength, you—"

"*RELENT.*"

Reverend Mickey nodded, leaned forward, gripped the podium. "Not bad," he said softly and the microphone cradled the softness. "But they are words, just words. The basic idea has got to be, change the words into *action.*" He leaned further toward them. "An ice-breaker, I am seeking an ice-breaker. Someone who understands what on earth I'm talking about."

The lights along the wall came up and The Castle was bathed in a silvery glow, like dawn in the China Sea. Axelrod heard a rustle, a craning, and looked to the far aisle. A small boy in a dark blue suit, white shirt and silver tie was walking down the aisle. He clumped up the stairs to the stage, walked stiffly to the podium. Reverend Mickey shook his hand; the lights dimmed and the spotlight encircled the two of them. The boy blinked hard and Reverend Mickey whispered to him. The boy brushed his eyes and stepped onto a box. He looked around and Reverend Mickey at the edge of the spotlight nodded. The boy faced front. "Well," he said and the feedback boomed at him. He jerked back. Then he firmed his mouth, leaned forward and said in a silken voice, "Las night I hadda take care of my sister. She wouldn drink her juice so I hit her . . ." His face began to crinkle.

"Keep going," Reverend Mickey whispered.

The boy blinked. "Well, I pologize to Wanda."

"What else?" Reverend Mickey said.

"I were wrong an I admit it."

"What else?"

"Well . . . if she don't drink her juice nex time I won't hit her . . ."

"All right. You won't hit her. But in addition, you will not feel how?"

"Funny?"

"Try again."

"Wrong?"

"Again."

"Mad?"

"Ah. Good. But don't ask it. Come on now."

"I won't feel *mad.*"

A burst of applause. Reverend Mickey came to the podium and hugged the boy. The wall lights came on, the boy waved and scooted offstage. Reverend Mickey pointed at him. *"That's* what I call an ice-breaker. Do you get the idea?"

"Yes."

"Do you *want* the idea?"

"Yes."

"All right. Who will now *smash* the ice?"

A short, heavy woman in a print dress smashed it. She waved at her friends, grabbed the microphone with both hands and told about this supermarket clerk. He had under-charged her, she'd kep quiet. But that night the veal tasted awful. Well, the veal and lotsa other stuff was gone, but she were telling the world, and that clerk, if he ever made another mistake she would talk right up. *Either* way. *An*—glancing at Reverend Mickey—she would not feel high an mighty bout bein so honest. Another burst, plus oh beautiful, honey.

A junior high girl had copied her homework from a friend. Never again, plus she would straighten out her friend . . . A man with things on his mind, no excuse, had run a red light . . . A boy had mocked his grandmother in front of his cousin, well he *an* his cousin were the jerks.

Axelrod listened and watched. Each one grew a bit stronger, a bit louder, and after a while Reverend Mickey only had to nod briefly and say next. It was right after a man had belted his wife for calling him gutless and decided maybe he *should* look for a job that Axelrod did it. Or rather, his arm did it. As soon as he heard next, up shot the arm. And it stayed up even as he gazed at it. Even as he wanted to pull it down.

"Well now," Reverend Mickey said. "We have a friend with us. And he wants to make his contribution. Everybody say hello to Bunny Berigan."

"Hello, Bunny Berigan."

Reverend Mickey smiled his huge smile. "Please come up, sir. Have no fear. You are among friends."

He shook his head. But his arm stayed up. And now, suddenly, he had joined his arm. Only then did it drop slowly to his side. He heard himself saying, excuse me. Found himself sliding past the lady in Lupo's seat. Found himself walking down the aisle, climbing the steps, floating across the stage. Found himself at the podium. He grabbed it.

He looked out. Every face was fixed on his. You would think he was Gable or Power. He squinted. Standing in the back, behind the last row, was a girl who was a dead ringer for Juanita. He stopped squinting, leaned forward. The wall lights went out, the spotlight stabbed at him. Holding onto the podium, he could hear Reverend Mickey whispering: "The ball is in your court. You are the *boss.*"

He coughed, murmured excuse me, dipped toward the microphone, hit it, pulled back. Then easing up to it, he said softly: "Johnny Weissmuller is dead." His voice rushed through The Castle. An answering *ahhh* came back; he opened his mouth and his voice was stronger: "Yes, dead. I wonder if Maureen O'Sullivan knows . . ." The Castle was as still as the moment Lew Ayres reached for his butterfly on the western front . . . "Or," he said, "for that matter, Mia Farrow . . ." He paused. "In any case, he's gone. It's over."

"Ahhh . . ."

He gazed out into the darkness and he could see the sick, limping elephants. Heading west. He shook his head. "I would like to reveal," he said, "that on a number of occasions I dreamed of Maureen O'Sullivan."

A voice cut the darkness: "Sweet dreams, baby."

He nodded and said: "Also Elspeth Brownleigh. Numerous times." He gripped the podium harder. "You see, Elspeth was a dead ringer for O'Sullivan. She was also Queen of The Castle. In a blue bathing suit . ."

Stillness again.

"I . . . sent her birthday cards two years in a row. Unsigned. Lupowitz said that was incredibly stupid . . ."

Into the stillness: "The man were right."

He leaned on the podium and now cradled it. "Lupowitz was an enigma," he explained. "Very bright, very reasonable. Yet he was hooked on Buster Crabbe. When I told him his name was Clarence, his reply was, 'What's in a name?' "

Stillness.

He smiled faintly. His sigh filled The Castle. "Klein was another headache. Somewhat different headache." The smile turned bitter. "It was . . . fairly common knowledge . . . that . . . he was . . . making out . . . with Elspeth Brownleigh . . ."

Out of the darkness: "Hot chick."

"Yes," he said quickly, "yes." He stared into the darkness. "Idiot that I was I refused to believe it at first. But it was true. Lupowitz clued me in. He knew *every*thing." Pause. "I have never forgiven Klein. Or Elspeth."

"Ah, c'mon, man . . ."

"Never." He tracked that voice, glared at it. "He was hit at Salerno. It scrambled his head. His lecherous head. He's in a VA hospital in Brooklyn. I have never called or visited him . . ."

"Ah man . . ."

"No, *never.*" He gripped the microphone, swept the darkness. Some of the elephants were folding up, lying down . . . He leaned in. "I do not let go, I admit it, I don't. Klein. Elspeth. Mr. Werkman. He let me down and I have never forgiven *him.* He sat in his car in his garage when the Germans moved into Poland. Turned on the motor . . . It is one thing to be a pacifist, it's another to throw in the miserable *towel* . . ."

"Shoot, I throws it in ever day . . ."

He straightened up. "To each his own," he said firmly. "My first wife. She loved concerts, opera. I went with her.

Many times. She would *never* go to the fights with me. She said it was sadomasochism on my part . . ."

"She say that about the fights?"

"Yes."

"Oh man."

He nodded. "My second wife called Churchill an imperial anachronism. So long, Barbara."

Very softly, far back: "Man, that cat is crazy . . ."

"Oh? How's this? I haven't seen my son in fifteen years."

"Why not?"

"He ran to Sweden in '69. He called me a dupe."

"I break my kid's arm he call me a dope."

He smiled. "Exactly." He squinted to the back, to where Juanita's dead ringer was standing. "I'm working on my third wife. She recently issued an ultimatum: Get out of the past or get out of my life . . ."

"Don't you take that, man."

"Hush!"

He panned around the darkness. "I told her we shall see what we shall see." There was no answer, but the darkness gazed back at him. He could feel it, feel them. This was how Niven must have felt, corkscrewing down to no-man's-land, or Cagney staggering to the chair. Or Weissmuller, knife in his teeth, diving, diving . . . He leaned into the microphone and his breathing filled the Church of the Holy Word. "Well," he said, quietly, "he's gone. So is Lupowitz. And Clarence Crabbe. And Klein. He's in the funny farm but he's gone. Elspeth can keep him. In Scarsdale. She can put out for him in Scarsdale." He stared out; Axel, Lupo and Lion stared back. "Mr. Werkman is gone. The man who said *never* despair. Lupo and I pulled him out of his car."

He was breathing into the microphone. "My father
. . . pulled me out of Townsend Harris, said it was spoiling
me . . . sent me to Morris. I had to finish in a *regular* high
school." He was breathing. "Well, Nathaniel Werkman is
gone. So is Lex Barker who was never even *in* the Olym-
pics . . ." Breathing. "I was in the band room. My father was
there. And Mr. Werkman. I played 'I Can't Get Started.'
You know what my father said? He said, 'You call that
music?'" Breathing, breathing. *"Twelve-year-old girls can swim
faster than Weissmuller."*

In and out he breathed. In, out, in, out. Then he
pushed off from the podium. Breathed in, threw his head
back, as far back as it would go. He cupped his mouth with
both hands and let it go. Tarzan's screaming yell smashed
through the dark stillness, bounced off the walls, the ceiling, the clouds, came back and filled the microphone, took
off again, and again, and again. And finally, as it died away,
he slumped against the podium.

The houselights came up. The congregation was on its
feet. The girl who was a dead ringer for Juanita was hurry-
ing down the center aisle. He was aware of advice, plenty
of advice:

"Repeal, brother!"

"Repent, brother!"

"Relent, brother!"

"Now, brother!"

He was aware of Reverend Mickey. He was aware that
Reverend Mickey was flashing him the fastest smile he had
ever seen. He was aware that Reverend Mickey was saying:
"Oh yes, oh yes, Mr. Berigan, oh yes. Welcome to the
elephants' graveyard."

He was aware that the girl who was a dead ringer for
Juanita was screaming: *"Don't you let him convert you, Bunny."*